Penny Loves Wade,
Wade Loves Penny

Penny Loves Wade,
Wade Loves Penny

Caroline Woodward

OOLICHAN BOOKS
FERNIE, BRITISH COLUMBIA, CANADA
2010

Library and Archives Canada Cataloguing in Publication

Woodward, C. Hendrika

      Penny loves Wade, Wade loves Penny / Caroline H. Woodward.

ISBN 978-0-88982-267-2

      I. Title.

PS8595.O657P45 2010   C813'.54   C2010-904421-5

We gratefully acknowledge the financial support of the Canada Council for the Arts, the British Columbia Arts Council through the BC Ministry of Tourism, Culture, and the Arts, and the Government of Canada through the Canada Book Fund, for our publishing activities.

Published by
Oolichan Books
P.O. Box 2278
Fernie, British Columbia
Canada V0B 1M0

www.oolichan.com

Printed in Canada on 100% post consumer recycled FSC-certified paper.

Cover Image: Marilyn Harris, www.marilynharrisart.com

Mixed Sources
Product group from well-managed
forests and other controlled sources
www.fsc.org Cert no. SW-COC-003438
© 1996 Forest Stewardship Council
FSC

For Jeff

best travelling companion

& home fire-keeper, too

"The end of all our exploring
Will be to arrive where we started
And know the place for the first time."

—T. S. Eliot

The first time…well.

I saw him swinging down from his truck beside the gas pumps. Someone yelled and he looked over his shoulder and smiled. Smiled, turning, shading his eyes with one hand, laughing and shrugging while our bulk fuel man walked over. I dodged behind the candy rack to get a better look. I couldn't see his face when he bent to fill the gas tanks so I looked at the truck. *Northern Gold Honey Farms*. A bright yellow banner unfurled by a gleaming swarm of bees across the green truck door.

From somewhere in the back of the Co-op, two buzzers rang. I used the intercom to call the boys to the loading dock and when I looked up, he was standing in the aisle with a wallet in his left hand, staring. Everything slowed down, every noise in that noisy place faded away to a white buzz, and I stared back at the blue flannel shirt, the black mop of hair and long, lean, blue-jeaned legs, and that curvy bottom lip parting from the top as if to speak and those green eyes, the clearest eyes ever. Whammo.

"Gas?" he got out. I managed to nod and turned to the till but the glowy, buzzy bubble effect stayed, swirling all around us. I zipped through the change clackety-clack, trying to slow myself down so when I turned to count it out to him, I could be normal and friendly and there you go, sir, thank you very much.

But I touched his hand, warm, not cold, not sweaty either, but warm and alive, counting out the change, and I lost my calm, efficient self, spilling all the coins and the bills too. He'd given me a faded red fifty. I looked up at those eyes, at the laughing spray of lines curving down the cheekbones, and that easy, kind smile, not the sneer or smirk most males between fifteen and fifty wear around here like a bad habit. I swam straight into those clear, bright eyes. Then I pushed myself away and held onto the counter with both hands.

"Well, fine eh? Very impressive," I said, scooping up the scattered money, my bitten-off fingernails scrabbling with thin dimes.

"Very," he said and I felt that soft voice curve right around the back of me and hold me snug at the hips. My knees wobbled and one bumped into the corner of something metal and painful under the counter. I took a big breath and leaned forward and smiled right back at him. We just flew at each other, both of us standing stock still. We wrapped ourselves around each other and flew right out the door of the Goodland Co-op Bulk Service Centre on that fine August morning, over his five ton truck, up into the perfectly blue beyond.

I linger when I daydream over that first time, scene by scene, my own home movie. Penny Loves Wade, Wade Loves Penny, a golden banner toted by swarms of happy little bees, unfurling across the endless blue screen. That's how I like to remember us.

Like that.

*   *   *

"C'mon, now, you're gonna be glad to see the backside of me for a week or so, admit it."

He gives her two more bear hugs, snuffling each side of her neck, getting one more good sniff in before he has to get going. Sleepy, Pears soap, soft housecoat.

"I'm happy to see your backside any old time, you big lug," she says, and grabs a handful of each blue-jeaned cheek, giving them a solid squeeze before moving her arms up around his rib cage. There she clasps hard, getting two quiet pops out of his mid-back. Driving, all that driving. They stand still, leaning into each other, listening to each other breathe for a while.

"You can expect a warmer house when you come home because I'm going to go nuts with that canned foam stuff for stopping drafts."

She swings one leg up behind him to wrap around his knees.

"What we really need, though, is for the flu bug to zap everyone at the school except me so I can be called in for a week of subbing. Hex the staff room for me, okay?"

"Will do," he says, snuggling closer. She closes her eyes and concentrates on memorizing the feel of his lean body against hers.

"It's good we put the storm windows up before you hit the road," she murmurs into his shirt pocket, stalling for time. "With a couple days worth of subbing every month, we'd be able to live here without worrying about a meal for the entire winter."

She gets a back squeeze now. Wade knows her wobbly vertebrae every bit as well as she knows his chronic slippage.

"I think you can splurge on a thing or two besides sugar and flour, Penny. We're not that broke, are we?"

He shouldn't have said that.

"Just make sure you send any cheques you get straight home, okay?"

She steps back, hands up on his shoulders, looking him in the eyes.

"None of this hanging on to them until you meander home. We've got tomorrow's payments covered, but nine days from now, it's the mortgage and machinery, a double whammy, which could wipe us out completely. We're usually way ahead of the game this time of year but..."

She shouldn't have said all that either. He steps away from her and picks up the battered stainless steel thermos and his coffee travel mug from the counter.

"We'll be okay. Not to worry, Pen. McCabe, Lafleur, Kowalchuk, Greene...those guys are good customers. They'll pay for the wheat I just trucked for them well before the 15th."

Looking over his shoulder at the closed office door, she says, "I'll look for those bills and remind them if they go over thirty days again. Okay, Wade?"

He says nothing, stares out beyond the walls of the house as if he is already on the road.

"Okay, Wade?"

*   *   *

Why's my head so filled with mortgage and machinery bill dates, hay bale counts, and all this nit-picking now? I'm squishing the juice right out of our farewell. Wrecking it. I don't want to argue with him, not now, not while I can feel his warmth. We're this far behind because his father stuck us with a pile of debt. I know that, damn it! And damn Morris a hundred times....Those guys'll pay us as soon as the Wheat Pool pays them, I know that. And that should be this week, or next. I just want to sit down at the computer and make up a proper receipt when they finally do pay us. Paid in full, by cheque, with thanks. Wade Toland Trucking, Ltd.

*   *   *

"Wade?"

"I'm just trying to think if there's anyone else who owes us for September work but that's it, the Big Four of Fairview. When do we get paid for boarding the new horses?"

"Middle of next month," Penny says.

"Good. We'll be okay," he says. "Honest."

"Okay," she says. I need to believe you, she wants to say, but doesn't. "Just put those cheques in the mail."

Penny hands over two, self-addressed envelopes, stamped special delivery.

"Don't worry so much. That doesn't help anything."

"No, I just…"

"Yeah, yeah, send the cheques. It's just money, honey!"

"Look, you're not the one getting the calls from our friendly bank manager and that grumpy new John Deere dealer."

Or the real estate agent who phoned and said he heard they were in the market to sell, just days after Morris' funeral. The one who stuck his business card in their door when they were away at the lawyer's office in town. Even after she'd told him they definitely weren't interested in selling, not at all, ever, he persisted. Pushing, working himself up into a lather.

"Okay, okay, I gotta get out the door here, Pen."

He gives her one dry peck on the cheek, followed by a tentative last hug shrugged off with a few pats. Casey prances outside the porch door, trying to decide whether to bark or whine.

"I'll phone," he says, back still turned, walking away, porch door flapping, his shoulders going up against the chill, bending quickly to ruffle the top of Casey's head. The dog stops then, sensing the mood. Departure. He turns to look at Penny, turns again to look at Wade now stepping up into the truck and then flops down on the scrubby patch of lawn, heavy head down between his front paws.

*   *   *

This is all wrong.

This isn't the way it's supposed to be at all.

"See you soon."

"Take care."

"Gimme those lips!"

"Love ya."

"You too."

"Bye hon."

"Bye."

That's how it ought to have been. Fond, affectionate, a bit clingy on both sides. Like that. Or like the time she turned back the kitchen clock three times to prolong his leave-taking, when she was pregnant the first time and didn't know it yet, and could not bear to see him leave for nine whole days, both of them red-faced and crying.

*   *   *

She watches the tail lights of the International move along the valley road until they disappear over Samson's Hill. A faint halo of light lingers high in the sky for nearly a full minute after he crests the summit. A nippy breeze skitters around her on the front steps, nips at her housecoat, ruffles her hair and makes her shudder. Summer's truly over and so is fall, for that matter. She heads back inside.

The mantle clock in the living room bongs once, the mellow note echoing through the house, soothing and familiar to her now. Five thirty a.m.

She doesn't want to go back to the lonely bed and she's already had one good strong coffee, at five a.m. with Wade. Her plan for today is to take advantage of the earlier than usual wake-up and tackle this draughty house. Not that she's complaining after twenty-four years in the bunkhouse with its three tacked-on additions. The Rabbit Warren. Dogpatch. She wants to try renting it out but Wade doesn't want other people on the property. She hasn't finished with him on that subject yet.

They have not had a holiday together, just the two

of them, for seven years, and that one hardly counted. Five days trapped in Reno with Morris Toland, trapped with her not-so-likeable father-in-law shouldn't count. It wasn't their pick for a holiday destination, not that they were asked. Then there was Morris handing them twenty dollars each after breakfast to go and gamble or see a show.

"Live a little, you two," he'd snorted, as if he doubted their ability to summon up a good time. Then he would ditch them until dinner, when they would eat good, cheap steaks together, before Morris resumed his evening's entertainment at the blackjack tables.

She and Wade had wakened early, enjoying long walks, gawking at the stretch limos and the hotels. Once they made it as far as the real desert, cautiously skirting the looming cactus giants and watching out for rattlesnakes, marvelling at this strangely familiar landscape, courtesy of Western movies. When the desert started to heat up, sucking out what little moisture was left in the air, they began walking back. They caved in and hailed a cab because they'd gone out too far and the heat was too intense for their pale northern hides. Then they went up to their air-conditioned room to watch a TV movie and to make slow, luxurious love. They had lounged in the lavender bubbles of their two-person soaker tub and sipped chilled, pale beer. That part of the holiday was very nice, the time hanging out together, and it didn't cost them much either. Neither of them had won a cent at the slot machines or roulette wheels they'd attempted playing during the first night in Reno. Neither of them felt entertained by losing money. In fact, after their short foray into big-time gambling, they hung on to their daily allotment from Morris. They spent the money on cheap meals for themselves and goofy little souvenirs and T-shirts for the twins.

Penny stares out at their former home less than fifty metres away. A reliable couple could rent the Rabbit Warren for two hundred dollars a month. Maybe that's too much, she thinks. Maybe one hundred dollars. Maybe that's too little. She'd have to find out more from other people, or read ads, since she doesn't know anyone else with this kind of arrangement. Anyway, as she sees it, her nice couple would be available to share the chores once a week, maybe Sundays, unless they're religious people. Fridays might be better. Unless they're Moslems, of which there are none that she knows of in Goodland. Saturdays are for Jehovah's Witnesses and Seventh Day Adventists but they all drive to their respective churches in Big Butte. Saturdays are also for practicing Jews, but the only one she knows is the high school math teacher in town, Rhoda Persky, who isn't overtly devout. Being a wonderful cook, she organizes special feast days mostly, for the diaspora of two dozen or so. They like the kitchen at the Goodland Hall and always rent it, despite the drive. The core congregation at the Good-land United/Anglican Church totals twelve adults and four children. No, the real upsurge in the local Christian population took place in the plain brown hall built by the new wave of evangelicals, outside of which are parked at least three dozen pick-ups and family vans on Sundays. Penny shakes her head.

Well over half of the Goodlanders she knows are

good-natured heathens who work seven days a week, like all farmers and ranchers have to do. If pressed, she calls herself a non-practicing Druid but she's learned not to quip about religion after being met with blank or coolly assessing stares a few times. Whoever rents the old bunkhouse, well, she'll sort out any Sabbath issues and respect their days of worship; and she'll happily share a big chunk of the garden with them as well. She and Wade can make weekends out of any two days of the week, go camping, go for a long drive, find cheap motels, anything, just to get away for a few days. Whoever it is they will be good people, say a nice young farm-raised couple starting out, or an older couple who've retired from farming, who don't want to manage a motel or an apartment block in the Okanagan, who don't want to leave the country life just yet, adjusting to being in a landless limbo. They would be people who were between things in their lives.

But if she and Wade pick their times away carefully, never leaving during calving or haying seasons, it certainly will be a lot less work and stress for them both. Especially on those days when Wade is away trucking and she has an early call to substitute teach...*and* she has to do all the morning chores *and* get out of their driveway onto the road after a metre of snow has fallen overnight. The new tenants will be expected to snow-plough the driveway first thing.

'How reliable can they be if they don't have a place of their own?' Wade fired off the last time they'd talked about it.

'Regular people who like animals and farm life and can run a few machines. People in good health who didn't inherit a ranch, maybe,' she'd said, cutting close to the bone for once even though saying so would set him off on a sulk. 'We'd check references, make sure that they weren't thieves or wing-nuts, for heaven's sakes!'

But he doesn't want to think about or talk about, much less do anything about renting the Rabbit Warren.

'You get to go away all the time,' she'd said.

'Yes, and that's why I like coming home and relaxing,' he'd said, 'I love how it always smells so good in our house after being inside that truck for days on end. And you always look so darn good as well, you little darlin',' he'd added, with his best leer.

Then, as if he finally remembered, 'You can go off and visit your family or your friends when I'm back home for a long stretch.'

Wade persists in thinking her idea of a holiday is seeing her family and friends without him. Her family and friends are scattered from Vancouver Island to North Carolina, not exactly a carefree weekend's drive from Goodland. For him the Peace River district of northern B.C. is at the centre, not on the edges of everywhere else.

'But that's not what I want! I want just us to go for a little holiday somewhere warm, by a lake in the Okanagan, or at the coast, by the ocean. Or help drive the kids to university or out to their summer jobs with their stuff like lots of other parents manage to do.'

She so rarely wants to leave the ranch but when she feels the urge, she really, truly, emphatically wants to be gone and he doesn't seem to recognize this one fact about her. Or else, and this she can barely admit to herself, he doesn't want to spend that much time relaxing alone with her anymore. Maybe they'll end up like those desperately bored couples who go out for dinner once a month and speak approximately twelve words to each other over the evening. The kind of tense and morose couple that other chatty and happy couples at neighbouring tables raise their eyebrows at, or wink to each other about.

But then she wonders why did he seem so content spending all those long winters together in their cramped bunkhouse quarters, warm beside the wood heater, both of them stretched out at either end of the couch, limbs entwined? Why did he seem so damn gratified, almost blissful, when they worked outdoors, side by side, through bitter cold mornings and afternoons? And why at nightfall did he embrace so willingly the monotony of feeding the animals, putting down more straw bedding in the two long lean-to shelters and the horse barn, keeping an eye on the ice situation in the water tanks. Why were these routines so happily shared?

She and Wade were enjoying, she thought, a kind of second honeymoon after the painful wrench of sending the twins off to their respective universities, now only seeing them at Christmas and at some point during the summers. Three long winters had passed without the daily chatter of Gwyneth's smooth alto and Gordon's rumbling baritone She missed their bantering in good humour, their sudden squalls. Penny made most of the dinners, Wade made most of the breakfasts; they each foraged for lunch and snacks but best of all, Wade did ninety percent of the dishes because he found the chore relaxing. This suited Penny very well. A man who liked doing dishes and made Sunday morning *huevos rancheros* was worth his entire weight in red onions.

No, she stops to think, it isn't that he doesn't like to spend time with me. That's silly. We tell each other everything, like best friends do. He comes home with his stories about places he's seen where he wouldn't mind living, interesting or outrageous people he's eavesdropped on, and spectacular scenery. He always says he wished I could have been with him, to see and hear what he had, but of course, somebody has to stay back home on the ranch and that somebody has to be me. For now.

She keeps her worries about fatal freeway pile-ups and mountain snowstorms and voluptuous waitresses to herself after he's teased her mercilessly about such fears. She doesn't mention the regular increase in mystery phone calls every single time he leaves on a long trip either. She suspects Evers, the luckless, creepy neighbour, but with no caller identification function on the old rotary telephones in both the bunkhouse and the old house, it could just as well be anybody dialling a wrong number. Couldn't it?

It could even be that smirking Mort Granger, who never fails to make a big production out of asking her where Wade is, always overly loud, in front of his cronies. Mort needs an audience, like a little banty rooster strutting his plumage in front of a gaggle of bored hens. She is unsmiling with him, playing it straight.

'Do you have a message for him?' she asks. And he never does. She knows that he knows damn well Wade isn't home. Why would he care anyway? He lives on a small acreage right beside the Co-op cardlock gas and diesel pumps with blowsy, bottle-blonde Lulu Gephart in her double-wide trailer and he doesn't farm a single bean. He works for the highways contractors, spreading gravel in the spring and summer and snow-plowing all winter. Penny has no doubt that he sees Wade fuelling up the International at the pumps before his long road trips and that Mort files the information away.

But it still doesn't answer the question, why on earth should the likes of Mort Granger care? Penny shakes off the annoying, petty argument escalating in her head, banishes the image of Mort's furtive little eyes and silly grin, and moves down the dimly lit wallpapered hallway to the kitchen.

She loves the big kitchen in the old house. The deep, enamelled sinks, the wood-burning Oval cookstove and the newer gas range side by side, the pale yellow painted walls, now in need of a fresh coat, and the pressed tin ceiling ten feet above. She even likes the Kelvinator fridge still humming away reliably after more than three decades.

There is just enough milk left for her latte and she pours it carefully into the stainless steel beaker. After putting it on a burner set to low, she goes to the sinks to wash their breakfast dishes and look out the windows where the faintest lightening of the inky blue sky on the horizon hints at sunrise in an hour or more. Anyone toiling at these double sinks has, in daylight, a panoramic view of the vegetable garden flanked by rows of raspberry canes, red and black currants, loganberries and gooseberries. Beyond the garden, a narrow alfalfa field pulls the eye to the rolling line of forested breaks on the far side of the Muddy River. In late April, she can hear the roar of spring run-off waters going down the coulee behind the barnyard, heading for the Muddy River. When the river breaks are covered in thousands of pale purple prairie crocuses in early May, they will take Casey and walk among them, picking a few and looking for wild onions and new sage amongst the tufted hairgrass and altai fescue and pumpelly brome. The subtle fragrance of acres of crocuses and the northern jasmine of silvery wolf willow make the first spring pilgrimage to the breaks a heady delight.

Penny shakes her head; standing over the stove, she keeps a close eye on the milk heating up. October already. Only a few scant weeks ago, morning sunlight flooded this kitchen, making every corner glow. She would like to add a sunroom to this room and then move the yellow and black-flecked arborite table into it, for breakfasts especially. The table has always been too small in scale for the kitchen itself. Penny suspects a previous Toland matriarch, likely Wade's grandmother, Amelia, had installed it in the early sixties or late fifties perhaps, tossing out the ruined walnut beauty Penny had discovered in the workshop, gouged and dented, probably from the spare parts that covered it.

Anyway, the arborite table, fashionable again in its cheerful, retro way, would look best in a much smaller sunroom, surrounded by thriving houseplants and three counters filled with flats of tomato and cabbage seedlings in early spring. Every fall, the air would be fragrant with drying bunches of herbs. Dill, thyme, oregano and wild sage. Baby's breath and windflowers— all dried and ready for wreaths and centre-pieces which she'd sell at the Harvest and Christmas Fairs.

She would look in the Buy & Sell or at the weekly auctioneer lists for a long wooden table, a Doukhobor or Mennonite-style built with sturdy, plain wood such as pine or birch. She wants one that will serve double-duty as a place to put her canning jars when the kitchen counters are already filled with quarts of peaches (two whole cloves or two leaves of fresh mint to each quart, four overflowing tablespoons of honey and then a slow pour of boiling water over the carefully packed golden halves). Then she'll find room for garlic dill pickles and tomato sauce, her three staples. They are the annual necessities, the must-do's, before the finessing of small, pretty jars of lime-zucchini marmalade, pickled beets and dilled baby carrots.

She contemplates the crunch of cauliflower, the snap of green beans, and the shock of tiny silverskin onions, all tartly dressed up together in mustard pickles. Or the small, savoured batches of red currant jelly, in jars glowing like rubies. This year she made half as much as she usually does every September with just the two of them rattling around in the place now. Still, she loves the work, making all the foods in the large and small jars, a gift of fragrant seasonal goodness. She loves the whole process from the early morning picking to the sounds of the canning lids softly popping into safe, sure suction on their glass sealers as she works at the massive wooden chopping block or the double sinks or tends to the blue-speckled canner steaming on the stove.

Yes, she will look until she finds exactly the right table, one generous enough to seat Gwyneth and Gordon and their future mates and her bright-eyed future grandchildren with Wade at one end and herself at the other. She will shove false modesty out the door and be adored for her rhubarb meringue squares and pumpkin pies made from scratch, her wealth of jams and jellies, and the *pièce de résistance*, the farm-raised roast turkey with wild sage and crab-apple stuffing. There will be a toast to good food on the table and good company having safely arrived, with Wade's finely flavoured, dry and slightly effervescent rhubarb wine for the grown-ups to drink and her sparkling pink rhubarb punch for the kids and teetotallers.

The milk in the beaker starts to foam over the sides and blue and orange flames flare up. The phone rings. Penny snatches the beaker off the burner, turns off the gas and runs over to the wall phone near the door. She glances up at the clock. 5:43 a.m. It rings again and then stops in mid-ring just as she touches it.

"Fine then," she says out loud and turns back to the stove. She pours the hot milk into the oversized pottery mug Gwyneth gave her last Christmas and then adds hot water from the tap to the beaker, setting it aside to soak. She uses the little battery-operated latte whisk, Gordon's stocking stuffer, to whip the milk into a froth and then pours in the coffee, adding a sprinkle of cinnamon on top.

She doesn't want to speculate. There are enough real things in their lives to worry about without giving up more than a second to fret about which local Romeo or wrong number from a faraway time zone caused their phone to ring at this early hour.

Where to start first? The chilliest rooms in the house are the upstairs bedrooms, Gwyneth and Gordon's guest bedrooms now, then the downstairs bathroom, and the entrance leading from the porch. Then she has to face the dark, dreary living room, originally the parlour, which had become Margaret Rose Toland's sick-room. It's rarely used except as a last resort guest bedroom with two dingy orange and brown plaid hide-a-bed sofas. Gordon's pals wouldn't mind crashing on them perhaps but Penny doesn't intend to put her mother or either of her brother's families in there. The place smells musty and something unidentified yet sickly sweet and decayed hangs in the air, enough to set her sensitive nose twitching. She suspects a long-dead, dried-up mouse trapped somewhere in the walls.

If money were no object, she'd have an enamelled blue cast-iron wood heater moved in on the north-facing wall and before it, a semi-circle of overstuffed armchairs. She'd rip out the tacky linoleum and find something light, like birch flooring, to put down. And she'd make hooked scatter rugs. Go for a warm Scandinavian feel.

She'd turn it into the library and games room, doing double-duty as a guest room, and she'd buy a really good quality queen-size hide-a-bed for guests. Or a Murphy bed, using that empty space on the east wall. Maybe add another tall window, triple-glazed, on the north side, and at least five more standing lamps.

Fantasy decorating aside, the room needs a good cleaning first—the walls washed, then repainted. At least she can afford the sudsy ammonia in hot water and her own hours of elbow grease.

She'll start with something small first, like the frigid bathroom downstairs. And right beside it, she'll investigate the tiny, stuffy home office, though it needs ventilation, she thinks. A window would do the trick. Then she'll go after the front hallway. The hallway is always chilled when the front door is opened, even with the extra barrier of the porch.

The long, covered front porch is a glorified mud-room, unheated and ugly. It barely hangs onto the house, behaving like a befuddled drunk, temporarily stalled as he sorts out his directions, swaying with the wind.

This porch is a matter far beyond the application of cans of insulating foam. It needs to be torn away from the house entirely and a proper cement foundation poured to stop it yawing away from the main building as the wooden posts underneath rot and crumble. Better yet, and completely beyond their budget, a new, insulated porch could be built on a cement foundation with wide, straight steps leading up to an elegant Victorian door which would be flanked by narrow stained glass windows. Inside, there would be built-in floor-to-ceiling cupboards where all the manure-spattered coveralls and coats could be hung out of sight of the discerning eyes and noses of urban relatives.

Most importantly, there would be enough hooks for every conceivable piece of harness needing repairs and for spare hats to be hung. Penny grins, sighs and finishes off her coffee. Time to stop dreaming and get to work. Casey needs his bowl of kibble and fresh water, first of all, so she quickly steps into the porch to feed their affectionate Mala-mute-cross, staying longer than she'd intended, giving him a good scratch along his woolly spine. Casey writhes happily, the tone of the new day restored to him.

Inside again, she shakes the can of insulating foam steadily and heads for the bathroom, to fill the tiny airspace under the window sill, which lets in a piercing, laser-like blast of near-zero air. On her hands and knees, she aims the nozzle at the source of the leak and presses down. Seconds later she uses her sharpest paring knife to trim the bulging dried excess away, flush with the wall. She runs the back of her hand beside it and *voilà*! The magic of foam insulation has done its work. No seepage of chilly air to ambush the damp and shivering escapee from the shower. The room needs one of those overhead heaters but she wants the wiring in this house inspected first. It had been wired back in 1962 when all of Goodland finally rejoiced in electricity.

She uses her hand to check for more drafts and finds another long, tiny seam to the right of the narrow window. It widens near the top and she feels another surprisingly wide band of frigid air puffing through in determined gusts. This window, she thinks, needs storm windows on both sides. The wretched thing was poorly installed to begin with. Or else old age and giving way to gravity was its lot in life too. She goes back to the kitchen to get the sturdy chair which always works best for getting her short frame up to high elevation tasks, like changing light bulbs.

Penny looks out the kitchen windows and sees two dust devils twirling side by side across the far side of the barnyard. The wind is up, no mistaking it.

Maybe I could teach quilting this winter, she thinks, but have the women come out to the house on a Saturday afternoon instead of me driving all the way to the school. Quilting pot holders and vests, baby quilts, family quilts, all kinds of Christmas present projects. Except we're too far away from town and none of the farm women around here do sewing and quilting any-more. Or want to pay me to teach them. Ever since her arrival in Goodland there has been a bit of that attitude towards crafts and there likely always will be.

'That new Toland wife, the substitute teacher, the one who does the handicrafts. What does she expect?'

'I can just order my bedding from Sears or go down to that new mall in Grande Prairie and save on taxes,' they'll chirp, with little sideways smiles.

I know very well what some of them think about my crafts and my canning and all of the stuff I love to do out here.

'All that Women's Institute old lady stuff. Just another garden slave, that Penny Toland.'

Well, she would tell them, I don't watch daytime TV and spend hours on the phone discussing the latest soap opera plot developments either. So there.

Think. Think! I can earn more in two days of sub-bing than I can from all the hours I'd put into six craft classes. So cancel that plan. Maybe she should just go into production for the big craft fair in town. Late November she thinks it is. Go for quick, cheerful and cheap as well as one major quilt. Do I have time, she wonders? Depends on subbing calls. Depends on whether she has enough fabric left to go into a major binge of sewing. It's been since last February when she finished the fundraising quilt for the choir. I need to check on what I've got packed away.

If I could get a half or three-quarter time teaching job and if he would just stay home and look after this place, we could cope with the bills. Trucking doesn't bring in enough money anymore with the way costs are going up unless he finds a way to do it smarter than his routine of four jam-packed months a year…when I hardly even see him around here.

When you come home this time, Wade Toland, we have to talk about stuff like this and make some changes around here or else we'll lose it. All of it.

Oh Wade, hurry home! You're being Mister Casual again. I pray you're not hiding something, just running away from it all.

Running away from me, too.

*   *   *

Wade sees Norman waiting at the Co-op parking lot, under the blazing yard light. As if that could keep him warm. His red canvas duffel bag sits on the pavement beside him. New white running shoes gleam on his small feet, now dancing from side to side. He's all bundled up in his brown leather bomber jacket, his shoulders up to his ears, while a huge grin lights up his creased, brown face.

"Wade! Sight for sore eyes, I'll tell ya! Colder'n'a witch's tits. Old weatherman wasn't lying last night. Yowzah!"

He shoves his duffel bag into the sleeper and smacks his paws together, warming them up. And they're off, after hooking up the double-jointed trailer parked behind the Co-op, carrying a full load of honey in barrels behind them. On the road. Officially.

"Carmina Burana, b-i-i-g music, mountain-scale music, ya gotta hear this, boyoboy, great stuff!"

Norman pops his new tape into the deck, cranks up the volume, and opens his stainless steel thermos.

"Cuppa java?" he hollers.

"Sure, thanks," Wade says, handing over his insulated mug, flipping the top off with his thumb. Norman fills up both travel mugs and puts the cover back on Wade's.

"A toast," he yells. "To the road!"

"The road!" Wade hollers back. They nudge the mugs together gently. Norman leans forward and turns up the volume again. Wade winces a little.

"Hey, ya get that rad looked at?"

"Ahh, hell. No, sorry, didn't get to it. Couldn't find a convenient time to get it into Red's Rads in town between my elevator runs. Tried for the best part of a week, just had to keep on trucking, you know how it is, then I'd remember again and start trying to book it but nothing worked. Just finished sixteen days straight of short hauls. Anyway, I topped it up with water and more antifreeze last night. We'll just have to keep an eye on it."

"It's all we can do. Go with the flow. Cope when ya gotta cope."

Norman wags his big head in commiseration, slurps at his coffee and settles back into the seat.

Wade just hopes the radiator holds up. As well as every last one of the eighteen tires, what with only two bald spares and one new one available as replacements. Not to mention the motor with more than 310,500 miles on it and many more to go.

They don't talk much on these trips, what with the constant rumble of the engine and Norman being more than a little hard-of-hearing. He said it had something to do with Vietnam artillery before he took the hospital plane home, got patched up, took medical leave and then hobbled across the Canadian border for good.

Norman settles back, unsnaps his jacket, and another smile spreads across his face as they head west on the Hart Highway with a big, red sun coming up behind them. As long as he's got good coffee in the thermos and good music on the tape-deck, he's a happy man.

Thanks to Norman, Wade now tolerates opera and has expanded his taste for classical music too. He finds, strange but true, that opera suits this landscape, all that drama with the Rockies looming on the horizon and the skies above swirling with cirrus clouds by day or dancing bands of lemon, lime and acid pink northern lights at night. And it isn't out of place to listen and look at the hundreds of undulating acres on either side of the Highway like it's a great quilt planted by a cereal-loving giantess. Here and there, minuscule men on toy harvesting machines move onto their fields, getting an start early. Wade hums happily as his truck roars by the earthbound men on their slow-moving machines.

Once the dew's off the wheat swaths, it's a rush to get it in the combine hopper or straight from the standing crop into the truck crawling alongside. Fuel up, grease up. Bale the last possible cut of hay, giant rounds of sweet-smelling protein. Wade knows that for each of them making hay while the sun shines is a gift, especially in October, It's a race to beat the first sight of an overcast sky, impending doom, early snow or icy rain. Screw the dew then, get the crop off any which way you can, but thank God all the while for the good weather. And pray. Pray hard for it to last.

The 1982 four hundred cubic inch Cummins engine purrs throatily beneath his hands and Wade looks ahead to the stony blue-grey slabs of the Rocky Mountains. He looks up at the royal blue morning sky and how it looks like the makings of a fine, cloudless fall day, at least on the eastern side of the mountains. He shifts in the deep bucket seat, manages an arched stretch, gets a pop out of his back, sighs, sips the strong coffee.

Just past the unincorporated hamlet of Progress, Norman climbs back into the sleeper to catch a few zees. He says zees and Wade says snooze. They have a comfortable routine going, Norman and Wade, after four years of long haul trucking together. They keep the truck rolling around the clock with two drivers. Better time, fewer expenses, less chance for perishables to perish on the home stretch. Wade shrugs his shoulders around and waggles his head from side to side to fix his neck. Now he concentrates on taking the truck down the long set of big, slow bends southwest to the foggy Pine River valley bottom, never sparing a glance for the brilliant gold leaves of the poplars, the burgundy saskatoon shrubs or the dark blue-green spruce covering the valley slopes on both sides.

With Norman in the bunk already, Wade knows he has to make it to Quesnel, at least. Maybe as far as 100 Mile House. Norman always drives the Fraser Canyon and the freeway into Vancouver. Wade would rather not deal with the congested traffic and the snarl of city streets so it works out well to share the driving this way. But he's tired already and that's not how he likes to start the longest trip of the year, the very last trip of the season. Wade's brain is jangling with shoulds and coulds and woulds.

He paws through the tiny cache of necessities in his shirt pocket, instantly recognizing a toothpick, a small rectangle of sugar-free gum and then, the bottle of eye-drops. The truck settles into a welcome straight stretch and Wade expertly drops the homeopathic elixir onto his eyeballs, topping them off with his sunglasses. He tugs his Co-op ball cap down even lower. The new day's sun is glazing the whole world in bronze and copper and bouncing the metallic shine straight into his tired eyes.

Over the past few years Wade's been happy to get away from the ranch and from the old man chasing after him twenty-four seven to do things his way. Phony old big shot, spending money like water the last twenty years but too cheap to get Mother a special bed so she could die in some kind of comfort. At least she wouldn't know about the mess the old man had left behind him. Sick old loser!

Shouldn't think ill of the dead. Well, it's too late for repairs on that score. Should have spoken up way back then. He wouldn't have dared hit me...I was too big for him, even at twenty-one. But I felt fifteen. Stayed fifteen to him too. Should have left right after Mom passed away, promise or no promise, should have taken Penny and made our life someplace else. Wouldn't have any attachments now. We'd just sell the place, pay off his debts and be done with it. But now, this way, it'll drag us down, take everything. Bankrupt us.

Wade turns the music down several decibels and passes a yellow school van packed with teenaged boys pulling out of Chetwynd. Off to Prince George, maybe, or Quesnel, maybe William's Lake. October. Volleyball season. Friday on the road, missing classes, life is good, hell, life is glorious for those boys.

Lucky them.

*   *   *

Penny sits down at the computer to read the latest contribution to the Goodland history book from Aloysius Deacon, the retired postmaster. He writes so well, she thinks, and his love for the subject is so palpable. His work rarely needs much in the way of her editing; but in fact, her eyes linger on the paragraph concerning the aftermath of World War I.

'The war dead left abandoned homesteads all over Goodland and their shacks were quietly visited and relieved of such goods as were needed or coveted by the visitors. The worldly goods of the dead soldiers, their thin mattresses, a few chipped dishes, any decent frying pans, blackened silver spoons, sepia photographs, letters and a few dozen books in several European languages were claimed by thieves, pack-rats, squirrels, mice, magpies and the weather.'

She sits still, thinking about the remains of two slab-sided shacks she and Wade used to ride near when they were first courting, the former homes of the Ueland brothers, both killed at Vimy Ridge. Goodland was settled in 1913 by Wade's maternal grandfather, William Horatio Good, and Grace Eugenia Pringle, who answered his ad in the *Western Producer* for a "housekeeper with intentions of matrimony". Gavin Toland survived the war, physically at least, and came to homestead in 1919 with his new bride, Amelia, the sister of one of his regimental buddies.

The history book committee had tracked down some of William Good's early letters to his family in England this past spring and now they planned to reproduce some of his handwritten script for the end-papers.

Today the Red Indians took me hunting for deer down the pack trail to the salt licks. They are very good shots indeed, one shot required, of course, but two, very rarely. I have a ways to go on that score but they are patient as can be with my fumbling about. Their Chief, John Greyeyes, is about my age and speaks a fair bit of English so we are becoming acquainted.

They do like to trade fresh game for any tea, sugar and pipe tobacco I have on hand and they are very fond of my fresh bread though they laugh a great deal about it. I think it's because I make it myself and this bachelor's competence in the kitchen amuses them. I especially like pan-fried prairie chicken

breasts rolled in flour, salt, pepper, a little of
our dried wild sage, some wild onions chopped
up, then pop them into a frying pan with hot
butter. Beats shepherd's pie hands down!'

Penny would like maps of the Pine Bluffs band's original berry picking and hunting routes to be included in the history book as well but she can tell that Edna, the formidable Edna Buford, is of the opinion that homesteaders are the "real" settlers, the ones who endured the northern prairie climate, patriotically reproduced and cleared their quarter sections of any trace of pack trails, pemmican caches or teepee poles, never mind suspected grave sites. Only the occasional black flint arrowhead still surfaces to remind them all of other times, other people long before them.

A collage of handwritten accounts from letters and journals would work very well on the endpapers and satisfy more people, Edna in particular. Diplomacy starts at home, as her father used to say, when she and her brothers were arguing about curfews or chores. Penny scrolls down the computer and finds the letter she had in mind, written by a man with a sense of humour, to his relatives in North Dakota in 1933.

'A steady stream of disappointed pioneers straggles out of Goodland these days, meeting bright-eyed newcomers en route. They exchange advice, some good-hearted and well-intentioned, some meant to dissuade or scorn those who

would put their health and few dollars to the test in this so-called paradise, the last Canadian homesteading frontier. In truth, by mid-winter, the milk is usually canned and the honey has yet to be discovered.'

Penny reflects on these hardy and desperate souls and applauds them all, imagining how they might advise her in her current travails. "Get out there and one or both of you find some decent-paying work!" "Sell off any stuff you don't use." "Get out of cattle. Sell the herd." And so on. She looks for the account of a family who spent their first winter in a cave they'd dug into the river bank. They'd arrived in November, of all months, and they somehow survived on turnips and moose meat and bannock and tea. She remembered reading a memorable line: "You can always make a meal out of frozen turnips but spuds, bah, once they're frozen, not even the dog will eat them."

*   *   *

Wade barrels through the Pine Pass, watching for the flashing legs of deer bolting across the highway and those of lethal, lumbering moose. Worse, other wacko truckers straying over the centre line, misreading a curve, cutting him off or just meandering motor homes sedately hogging the road. He has to stay focused in the here and now, eyes peeled, to get this rig through the Rockies. His eyes swing back and forth, up and down, soaking it all up, everything, he loves it. New day, new trip, new money coming in soon.

The hours flow by in a road rhythm of curves,

climbs, straight stretches and long and short hills. Clutch, shift up, clutch, shift down, braking only rarely. Wade breathes through his mouth when he meets the heavy chemical stink of the pulp mills, taking the truck route to avoid downtown Prince George, slowing to a crawl and finally stopping at the card-lock pumps to fill both of the hundred gallon tanks. Nothing but snores from the sleeper now. Wade smiles at the steady rumble and whistle. Norman has the great gift of falling asleep within minutes and staying asleep for hours thereafter.

Wade drinks water and finishes an apple as he drives southward, to blaze along the nearly deserted autumn highway, newly paved and straighter than ever. He spots three glossy black bears in three separate locations, each one gorging on green oats, a reseeded bonus on the late fall fields. Overhead a cloudless sky shimmers over the fields and dense forest which gives way to ranch country, the Cariboo's split-rail fences and its many-coloured cattle. Angus black, Charolais cream, ivory Limousin, white-faced Herefords with coppery hides, brindle rodeo stock Brahmas, surly and hump-backed, one rare black and white Holstein. This isn't gentle dairy country.

He always thinks of Penny when he sees the horses. She'd be pointing out the spotted rumps of the Appaloosas, showy brown and white paint ponies, their equally flashy black and white pinto cousins, sorrel beauties with Arab showing in their fine, arched necks and sweet, dishy faces, here and there some big Belgians and Percherons, logging skid-horses probably, as well as glamorous blonde Palominos, the rodeo parade favourites, and the heavy-haunched intelligent Quarter-

Horses, the plain brown working cattle horse without parallel, the Border Collie of the horse world.

Wade is smiling now, seeing Penny in his mind's eye, stretched out over Maggie-May's bright sorrel neck and himself clomping along behind on old Ben Brown, racing each other to a certain tree or a fence-line or the home gates. She sticks to any horse like a burr, cooing in their ears, and it is a mutual love affair. He is merely tolerated, provided transportation by them for as long as he comes along with her.

His rig keeps rolling, rolling, past Quesnel and Williams Lake, the lumber and ranch towns, past the lakeside resorts and the massive log b&b's and their *Wir sprechen Deutsch* signs. Steadily roaring southwest past abandoned gas stations and derelict house trailers, toward the sagebrush desert hills of Cache Creek. Onward to the jagged stone edges of the Coastal Mountains, the seething jade rapids of the Fraser River carving through them, bellowing down the narrow asphalt band of Highway 97, clinging to its manmade shelf above the great river.

Norman snores in the little cave behind the thick cloth curtain and then wakes up after six dreamless hours. He reaches for the calculator in his shirt pocket and silently works through a rapid series of figures. He smiles, tucks it back in his pocket, closes his eyes and waits for the wake-up call.

Wade paws through his small soft-sided cooler for roast beef, sweet onion and horseradish sandwiches during another rare straight stretch, finding them tucked beside an icepack. He wolfs down two halves, finds a slab of carrot cake topped with cream cheese icing, his favourite, and washes it all down with the last cup of coffee from the thermos.

He drives on, oblivious, caffeinated, beset by his own yammering group of demons, so afraid this is the year his life will take a final turn for the very worst, that Penny will finally see him for the fiddle-footed excuse for a man that he thinks he is. Okay, he was a decent, patient father at least, not like his own old man, the hypocrite, but he's not got much else going for him really. With no kids at home to make him feel useful anymore, he feels like a loser adrift. Two good kids, smart like their mother. He muffles a cinnamon-coffee-horseradish belch and with his eyes still glued to the snaky set of curves ahead of him, he finds the roll of antacids in his shirt pocket.

Penny. He sends her a telepathic one-armed hug and a kiss on top of her sandy brown head for thinking of his favourite sandwiches and his favourite cake. Then the little pang hits him. She's stuck there, working on the books maybe. Big bills to somehow pay, two sets of university costs to help out with, next to impossible re-mortgage negotiations, thanks to the old man, rotting away with a smirk on his useless skull. Penny, worrying day and night, her nerves fraying. Working overtime on overdrive, canning, cleaning, digging, sewing, feeding, hauling, driving off to whichever school has called her in, dressed in her school teacher clothes. Driving off in the not-so-dependable 28 year old Dodge Dart with her emergency flashlight, extra socks, a candle and a spare sleeping bag. Just in case.

His jaw clenches in a frown and he hunches over

the wheel, not noticing the accordion effect on his spine, not yet. His bladder finally alerts him to the here and now and he gears down to pull into a conveniently placed roadside rest stop, one with a deluxe solar-powered Bill Barlee's Biffy—so named, unofficially, by members of the grateful travelling public, for the M.L.A. who sponsored these new-fangled toilets to replace the smelly old ones. Wade leaves plenty of room for a grocery freightliner heading north to swing back out onto the highway. He wakes Norman then (at least he assumes he's woken him) and both of them head for the bathroom, do the tire check, and switch drivers.

Wade climbs back to rest while Norman handles the narrow, winding highway through the Canyon, plunging through the series of tunnels, Alexandria, Sailor Bar, Boston Bar, and the rest, all a blur, keeping pace with the freight trains flanking the highway, heading east and west. After getting past the outskirts of Hope, he enters the fray of the Fraser Valley freeway.

Norman pops a Kronos Quartet CD, 'Caravan', into the player and lets the mood overtake him, lets his eyes, alert with rest and resolve, dance over the backs of the civilian vehicles below him, saluting fellow big-rigs. He revels in his jaunty flowing traffic mood, the lovely, lovely music, and joins the motley cavalcade heading for the Pacific coast, taking the Number 10 highway through Cloverdale, Surrey and Delta to avoid down-town Vancouver. He copes a little better than Wade with the crazy, fast, or just plain bad city drivers, more and more of them and getting worse every trip.

"Dumb fuck!" he bellows, after a near-accident jars

him out of his musical driving reverie, glaring at the brand-new coppery SUV, the driver's hand still holding the tiny cell-phone, lurching to the left after wandering into Norman's lane.

"Shit for goddamn brains!"

*   *   *

It's not that bad I try and tell her, but she's not listening.

We might have to sell she says and her lips tighten up.

She's losing her looks, my little Pen is, when I inspect her close-up. It's the bad haircut. She's been leaning over the bathroom sink and hacking away with a pair of kitchen scissors, trying to save money on Marcy's twenty-two dollar haircuts. The worry lines are getting deeper across her forehead and there are more small furrows between her eyes. She's skin and bones too.

Don't be land proud, I say. I'm not and it's my family's land.

Her lips get thin and her eyes go hard. And your mother would be sickened to hear you talk like that she says. But she doesn't ever say that. I just think that's in her mind whenever she gets on my case about money. All she has to do is mention money and I fly a little off the handle, try to back her away from the touchy spot.

But she knows me now, she doesn't back off. Some show of my temper might fend most people off but not her; she's like a wiry fox terrier going after a weasel.

Where's the invoices?

I dunno, I say in a bored kind of way, like I've got more important things to find than frigging invoices worth four thousand bucks to us. I play dumb and it drives her nuts.

We stare at each other for one long beat, glaring full force and then turn away. Not reaching out to place our hands on either side of the plexi-glass. We won't touch each other for days and we wouldn't, even if we could, now.

*   *   *

Booming horns in the salty fog, sea gulls shrieking, saying something, saying something, wake up now, wake up!

Wade opens his eyes, groggy, smells the dense sea air and smiles. They made it. He checks his watch. Sixteen hours flat from home to the Pacific Ocean. Even the weight of the air is different here, like hand lotion all over his dry northern skin. He can breathe easier here.

He can't hear the motor and yet he can hear other motors all around him. He struggles up to his elbows and peers out of the curtains to confirm his hopes. Ferry terminal. Fine, good, exactly right. He swings his head the other way. No sign of Norman but he spots the lights inside two phone booths across the parking lot.

He pulls his boots on and ambles over, fishing his phone card out of his battered leather wallet. He tries once but it's busy. He stretches both arms up to hold the top of the booth and brings them down the framework, getting them to a 'Hands up' position. He leans in and his upper back pops twice.

"Oh, my," he groans, blowing out spent air. "Oh, my."

He tries to call home again but it's still busy so he walks over to the bathrooms and splashes cold water over his face, clamping a wet paper towel to the back of his neck. Outside again, he takes in a big lungful of the cool salt air, smiling at the row of swaying baskets with their waterfalls of bright flowers cascading down in a tropical abundance. He loves it all. Even when it rains, it's like a misty dew coating the leathery leaves of the arbutus and the needles of the giant Douglas firs and the primeval ferns, a world of exotic difference from the silt-filled rivers and long, cold winters and frost-blackened September gardens of home.

Wade tries to call home six more times but the line stays busy. The amplified voice of the ferry terminal system urges everyone bound for Vancouver Island to return to their vehicles in preparation for boarding. Time's up. He'll try again on the other side or better yet, see if one of the ferry phones is available. It's getting harder just to find a public phone, what with everyone and their dog having cell phones. Norman's back in the driver's seat and Wade climbs up into the passenger seat beside him.

*   *   *

Penny thinks she hears the kitchen phone ring again just when she's emptied the fifth can of insulating foam. But after straining her ears for thirty seconds, she hears only the intermittent whistle of the wind rushing around the house. She's worked her way up to the attic, which used up two full cans, from the second floor where she discovered she could actually feel a thin slice of the northwest wind entering from inside one of the bedroom closets.

She walks down the narrow wooden stairs to the main floor and the dismal living room. It seems draft-free but the ceiling is so high that it still feels chilly. There is one grate admitting tepid warmth from the ancient oil furnace below. She'd turned down the thermostat earlier so that she wouldn't miss drafts, or be misled by warm air from any of the grates. This particular room needs light and warmth and laughter and love, all of it to banish the musty dankness that clings to it like a glum ghost, she thinks, and not for the first time. It isn't the ghost of Margaret Rose Toland either, even though she spent the last four months of her life in here. It's somebody else. Penny shakes her head. Fanciful imaginings aren't a good thing to indulge in all by oneself in this house.

This time she isn't imagining it. She runs for the phone in the kitchen, heart thumping happily. The timing is right. He must have boarded the first big ferry just now and can take a breath, some time to call home.

"Hello, Penny? This is Georgie. How are you doing?"

Penny sags against the counter and wearily hitches herself up to sit on the high wooden stool below the wall phone. She puts the spray can down and picks up a pen and the small stapled pad of reused paper. She gets through the preliminary pleasantries.

"I'm calling to ask if you'd be able to come to a meeting next Tuesday afternoon at one o'clock, down at our place? Edna thinks the Historical Society needs to get back into gear again, meet face to face, and plan the final four months of the book. Can you make it then? We really need you there so I'm phoning you first."

"I can do that, Georgie, but if I get called for subbing, you know I'll have to cancel at the last minute. I'm sorry but that's how it is, as you know."

"Of course," coos Georgie. "We understand. And we know you've been way too busy this past while as well, you and Wade both, with so much to look after. Why, Bert told me that Wade worked sixty-one days in a row this summer and fall, with no time off, not one day! He heard that from one of the radiator shops in Big Butte the day after Wade tried to get the big truck looked at during one of his elevator trips to town. You two both deserve a little time off or a real holiday soon. Well, I wish you all the best and a good evening and hope to see you Tuesday, but we'll understand completely if you get called in to teach. Bye, bye now."

And she's off to the next name on her telephone tree, doing Edna's bidding, as usual, though with a bit of her own freelance gossip elicitation thrown in. Penny was too tired and disappointed to offer up any information to Georgie regarding Wade's time off though it gives her pause to hear it from someone else. Sixty-one days straight. She feels ashamed of her own ingratitude, of her own self-centredness, really. Persistently imagining Wade as footloose and carefree just because he's away from the ranch, not seeing him as he really is, driving day after day for two months, trying to squeeze in a booking at the garage and being unable to, keeping that truck—and himself—running so hard he is skimping on maintenance. She sighs again, heavily. Too soon old, too late wise.

Packing up her seven year old desktop computer with the tall tower and the awkward bulbous monitor is a real pain. If she comes into any money, she'll get a brand new laptop and that will make her life as the secretary of the Goodland Historical Society much, much easier.

It is nearly done, she reminds herself...three years worth of gathering material for the book, due out next spring, the long-awaited history of Goodland, all its quarters and sections, family by family, from the first homesteaders to newly arrived Big Butte commuters. Georgie Lemieux has written the First Nations history, with the help of one of her grand-daughters, a lawyer and the Chief of the Pine Bluffs Band. It's Penny's favourite contribution so far, that and the letters of William Good, first settler, first postmaster and organizer of the Co-op Store, Wade's maternal grandfather. She loves the whole cumbersome endeavour and the stalwart group of six women and two men who have tackled the overwhelming task of cajoling histories of no more than 750 words each out of everyone.

But her job, as the editor, is the most difficult. She agreed to it only on condition that each edited history would be sent back to every person who submitted it for their final approval. She had no desire to be viewed as the only censor or axe-wielding editor of vital (or, usually, the not so vital) family information on the committee. After the first three histories she worked on met with whole-hearted approval from all parties concerned, the group stood solidly behind her and she no longer worried about being hung out to dry for errors or omissions, which might take several generations of a family to grant her forgiveness if not absolution. It was a revelation to Penny, who did not consider herself a writer with much flair, to discover she could diplomatically shape and nip and tuck and help each person deliver a family history of which they felt very proud. She aimed for each writer's authentic voice to come through and she let each of them know that she didn't want a stilted Grade Six essay of potted history. She wanted warts and all and if no one was willing to write on behalf of the family, Edna Buford herself went after the reluctant chroniclers for other documents and came up with significant letters and telegrams and photographs. Eventually, nearly everyone in Goodland was jollied or browbeaten into contributing to the forthcoming *Goodland: A Century of Community.* Penny smiles as she heads back to the problematic room in this family's house.

The oil furnace needs to be replaced by a modern gas and wood combination. She kneels beside the living room grate, trying to warm her hands. Gordon, even though he no longer lives at home, is keen to experiment with solar and wind and geothermal energy. Even if they could afford all the start-up equipment, Wade doesn't seem interested in taking a chance on any of it. She's never had an oil furnace before and now she has to deal with this outdated beast in the cellar. This reminds her of the filters and her promise to herself to check them and see if Morris left a record of when they should be changed or cleaned or whatever it is that has to be done to them.

Her energy is flagging. It is nearly 7 p.m. The chickens and weaner pigs have been fed and Casey has had his bowl of kibble as well. Her own dinner was a reheated bowl of ham and bean soup with a grilled cheese sandwich at 5 p.m. She cannot detect any drafts around the living room windows or anywhere else in the room after doing a slow patrol. She cannot force herself to work any longer and so she stops, halfway down the stairs to the cellar. The dirt floor of the root cellar is to the right and the partial cement floor, where the furnace stands, is to the left. One bare light bulb dangles near the bottom of the stairs. She realizes that she wants a flashlight before going any farther into the dingy hole. That decides the issue.

The furnace filters can wait one more day. She's beat. And she will not force herself to wriggle into the furthest reaches of the crawl space down here either, for fear of setting off an old packrat trap or finding some critter, dead or alive. She shudders, thinking of the rats and wintering garter snakes. Then she hears the phone.

She rushes back up the stairs and shoves the heavy door behind her to trap the dank potato sprout air below. Even with her lined denim chore jacket on for extra warmth, she's chilled. Her feet, in thin socks and beat-up running shoes, and her bare hands especially, are freezing. She grabs the phone after the fifth ring.

Mother. Give me strength. She's off like a Gatling gun with a British accent, as Morris used to say.

"Just thinking of you, Penny, thought I'd call, it's been a while, see how you are up there. All ready for another cold winter in that big old house, are you?"

"Oh, fine," says Penny. "Busy, you know, cleaning,

winterizing. Moving over here took most of the summer, bit by bit, but at least we had help from both of the kids before they left for university again. All their stuff is in boxes in their new rooms so I don't need to do anything with it. Oh, and Wade left for the coast early this morning for his last long haul of the year, the one with all the honey."

"Well, why didn't you come down with him? We could have had a nice visit, just the two of us. You could have stayed right here with me while he did his deliveries. Surely you can afford hired hands now that you've got that Ponderosa estate all to yourselves! Think about it for next time. I haven't seen you for two years, almost. I do keep track, you know. Saw both your brothers and their families this summer when they came out but I've told you all about that I guess, right after the time Morris passed away. So, don't you feel like you're rattling around in that big house? How long is he gone for this time? Aren't you just a bit afraid all by yourself out there?"

Penny heaves another sigh, covering the phone. She can rarely get a word in edgewise with her mother but she manages to explain that she can't just drop everything and leave home as if they only lived two streets apart. It's 1200 kilometres one way but Gladys Brown, schooling done at age fourteen and sent off to clean other people's houses by her own domineering mother, has never learned to read a map or drive either. She is Without Clue One, as Gwyneth would pronounce of one of her hapless suitors or dull teachers. Gladys rattles on about her favourite grocery store closing down and how she and a friend have to take the bus to get to the mall where they both get lost in an enormous store not nearly as good as their neighbourhood one was, just an easy walk away, one and a half blocks.

Penny is still stuck on Gwyneth. She imagines not being able to see her own daughter for two whole years, knowing it may soon be likely, given her daughter's adventurous streak. Her throat lumps up and her eyes flood with tears. She mustn't give anything away. She murmurs with a perky 'mmm-HMM', after each of her mother's phrases. When Penny calms herself down, and Gladys pauses for air, Penny offers news: the garden being done for the fall, except for the pumpkin patch, the cattle, nearly two hundred of them, and their small herd of twenty horses, seventeen of them paying boarders for the winter, all of them now up on the fenced and cultivated land, after a summer of ranging below on the leased uncultivated land on the river breaks.

She knows Gladys loves hearing about all their animals and their crops and for the first time in a long while, Penny softens and prattles back at Gladys, giving her what she wants, a chatty overview of her life. Penny knows that what Gladys really wants is more fodder for her conversations with her card-playing friends, something new to add about her adult children and grandchildren. What Penny loathes is her mother's ghoulish streak, her lust for bad news, even at the expense of her own family, all of them busily living their own lives far away from her, all of them raising a toast at their own get-togethers, glasses held high to honour long-dead Albert Brown, their patient and good-natured father who ran interference when Gladys was overwrought, which was often. But today, Gladys seems chipper, upbeat even. Penny goes on to reassure her about Casey, now two years old, a loyal one hundred and twenty pound Malamute-cross, good company with a deep, fierce bark when he does decide to bark.

What Penny doesn't say is that she's spent a lot of time alone in twenty-four years and that she has the phone and common sense and the shotgun to scare off black bears or thieves or worse, as a last resort.

"Well, does Gordon like vet school? Not always pleasant work, mind you. Having to put down people's pets and give out bad news, just like doctors but you know how people are with their pets. I just can't have them anymore. Too hard on me, really, when they have to go. And Gwyneth still set on teaching, is she? Will she get a job, I wonder, with all these cutbacks? You just never know, do you? We're heading for tough times again, oh, I certainly think so. Wouldn't she be better off going into nursing, with everybody getting old and all that? That's what they all say now, don't they, look after the aging population, that's the future of the job market. Well?"

Penny smiles. Her mother refers to 'everybody' else aging, excluding herself with her Maggie Thatcher helmet of sprayed auburn hair of course. Penny stays relentlessly positive about the twins, talking about their jolly roommates, how convenient it is for them to get to all their classes in Saskatoon and Vancouver, respectively.

"Why, I wouldn't be surprised if Gwyneth went off to teach in Inuvik or Africa or Korea," declares Penny, cheerfully flapping the conversational red cape. "And Gordon has two more year to go, of course, but he's always in the top five percent of his class. He's wanted to be a vet since he was twelve so we know he'll land on his feet wherever he sets up a practice."

If she were to let down her guard, reveal the slightest doubt about her children, Gladys would pounce on their grievous potential for failure with that strange, triumphant note of pity and glee in her voice. Gladys is, as Margot, Penny's smartest sister-in-law, detected within ten minutes of meeting her, jealous of her own children. She perceives them as having easier lives than she ever had, lives with more money, more labour-saving appliances, more education, better-behaved children and more doting spouses, and that they have had the colossal nerve of benefiting most from her ordeal of immigrating to North America. Except, of course, for Penny, who chose a rancher and an isolated life of hard labour in the north when she could have found a well-paid teaching job ("with all those holidays!") close by, living in a civilized city. 'It's always all about her, of course,' noted Margot, who didn't miss much.

If Albert were alive, he'd say in his mild-mannered way, 'Well, dearie, what else did we cross the Atlantic for? Certainly to make sure our children had more opportunities than they would have had in Liverpool, as we have had ourselves, owning our own plumbing business, not having to doff our caps to the lords of the manor or anyone else, right?'

It took Penny until she was nearly forty years of age to realize that her own mother was still around thirteen years of age inside, thwarted and petty, incredibly stubborn and utterly convinced by her own point of view. Gladys believed that men should provide and that women should raise the children (even if they didn't really enjoy them all that much). Women ought to keep the house tidy and clean, supper on the table at six sharp, and the reward? To dress up with one's hair freshly set and immobilized with half a can of hairspray for a proper Saturday night on the town. Bowling, darts, a movie, a nice dance, or meeting friends at the Legion for a pint, and definitely not in a cavernous Canadian excuse for a pub, all that Ladies & Escorts nonsense in the 50's from which she has never recovered.

Penny's mind is at sea, floundering, snagging on reefs of accumulated judgments etched by long-gone acidic froth, and besides, she urgently needs to go to the bathroom. Gladys is cheerfully going on about a whist drive with her widow's club tomorrow evening. Penny wishes her luck and hangs up quickly, feeling ungracious.

The phone rings again.

A long distance crackle and hum and some sort of loudspeaker...? Whoever it is hangs up before she can even manage hello. She worries for a few seconds, waiting for a second call before she heads down the hall to relieve her insistent bladder.

Wade the Wanderer. Stuck in an early snowstorm in the mountains. Truck flipped over, eighteen wheels spinning in the air like a dying red and black water bug, tons of honey pooling on the road. Amber honey and blood in swirls on the pot-holed grey pavement.

Knock it off!

But she hangs around the kitchen, waiting for the

kettle to boil for a small pot of spearmint tea, picking dried foam off the can, waiting, really, for another ring. She imagines Wade in a phone booth. Phone out of order. She'd vetoed a cell phone after hearing horror stories from other Goodlanders about them costing double and triple what had been advertised. Even worse, half the north country and certainly their highway through the mountains were without reception and service when you needed it most anyway.

There is no budget at all for mechanical disasters. He has nothing to spare except fifteen bucks a day for hot coffees and fast food, with the diesel fuel put on their wheezing credit card. She'd packed the cooler and the plastic picnic tub with enough food for a week as well.

Then there's Norman and who knows where he might want to stop on this trip? He might go for steakhouses and bourbon, for all she knows of the man. A real sleaze-ball, she thinks. Phoney baloney and he knows that she has him pegged as such and he won't even look her in the eye either. She wishes that Wade would find somebody else for the long hauls to drive with because as far as she is concerned that Norman is just a loud-mouthed b.s.'er!

Penny takes a deep breath, calms herself down from another useless hissy fit about Norman. She wants Wade to be spared any expensive screw-ups on the last trip of the season. This is the haul that will get them through the winter, ahead even if nothing else goes wrong... and if she gets at least five day's worth of subbing every month. Five days. That's not too much to hope and pray for, is it? It's a lot though, and she knows it.

Still, it's very odd to miss that call and she's positive she heard the phone earlier too, before her mother and Georgie got through. Penny mentally tours the phone locations: the kitchen, the outdoor shop and office. *The office.* She quickly steps into the room beside the kitchen and goes to the oversized desk that takes up a good third of the tiny space. The old-fashioned answering machine hulks on the top right-hand corner and the first thing she notices are the strands of charcoal grey cassette tape bulging up and out of its innards. She untangles the mess and removes the spent cassette. No wonder the thing hasn't been picking up messages. She's used this phone less than ten times since they moved in a month ago. The last time she checked the answering machine was a week ago, after coming back from town.

What if she missed something important, something about the kids or Wade or anyone in the family? Who else has been trying to reach her today?

This is when she realizes she is one step away from being inhabited by the same mind-set as the woman who spends her days and evenings in her triple-locked Vancouver home, watching floods and tornados and prison riots on the television that is turned on first thing in the morning and which stays blaring on through to Gladys' bedtime. Ever anxious to phone her middle-aged children with queries about the weather in Regina, Toronto or Goodland before launching breathlessly into the natural and man-made horrors of Detroit and New Orleans and Coquitlam. A catastrophobe. What Penny has always dreaded becoming after a certain age, consigned to idleness and endless T.V. in a rest home. But then, living on the ranch means never retiring, officially, barring ill health. Never being bored either, with all the things to do, indoors and out, four seasons of the year. If the call is truly important, the party would have phoned her non-stop today.

This is also why it's so important to get away from the land once in a while, to see what other thoughts are in her head besides worrying like this or worrying about making a living or doing chores or balancing the bank book or worrying about helping out the kids more...

Casey is barking, getting louder, very insistent. She hears heavy footsteps on the porch and springs out of the kitchen chair, still clutching the foam can. The powerful yard light illuminates the black pick-up parked outside their pole gate. Hell and damn! I wasn't paying attention to the dog. Now what?

He knocks very softly. Casey growls, doesn't let up. She takes her time, at least a minute. He knocks again, twice. When she opens the door, he is halfway down the steps, exactly where she wants him.

"What's up? I've got my hands full in here."

She pokes just her head out around the door so the piggy little eyes of her neighbour can't roam up and down her body. Sherwin Evers is the one person on earth she can be rude to right off the bat without feeling ashamed of herself.

"Oh, hey there, Penny! Well, nice enough day, eh? I thought you'd be home...I kinda thought I'd drop by and let you know if you need anything, anything at all, just let me know. You know I'm not that far away, night or day. Say, Wade doesn't have any use for that chop mill of Morris' now, does he? I was thinking if..."

"Gee, it might be better to ask Wade about that. I'll get him to call you sometime. Gotta run now. Bye."

He trudges back out to the gate that he couldn't be bothered to open, big shaggy head swinging around from side to side, taking in the neat row of farm machinery flanking the barnyard road on the left and the half-acre garden to the right. He inspects it all blatantly and doesn't miss much. Casey is skulking low to the ground ten feet behind him, discreetly herding him back to his battered black, half-ton truck.

Good dog.

She knows he didn't open their gate and drive up to the house out of any reasonable concern. No. He'd rather take his silent walk and get a good snoop in. The chop mill is in the small machine shed, protected from the weather, well out of sight. So how does he know it's even there? Wait till she tells Wade about this, the very day he leaves. She's ranted on to him about Evers having a telescope fixed on their place. Every summer there is a high rate of coincidence between her wearing shorts while hoeing the garden and Evers roaring down the hill on some pretext or other. That, and the fact that he never visits when Wade is here by himself. When she's away from the place, teaching or whatever.

"Thou shalt not covet thy neighbour's wife nor thy neighbour's ass, nor, specifically, thy neighbour's wife's cute little ass," said Wade only once. She had whipped him over the shoulders with a tea towel and he promised to grow up eventually. It was easier to laugh it off when the two of them were here. Problem is, she thinks, I get spooked when Evers arrives within hours of Wade driving away. It happens too often for my liking and I'm never quite prepared.

Prepared for what? Telling him exactly what she thinks of him after knowing him for more than twenty years? Greedy, envious, lustful, sneaky, the list goes on. No, all she can do is maintain a very thin veneer of politeness and fend him off, time after time. She'll never forget him and his shaggy-haired cousin coming in for coffee at the Co-op counter and the pair of them staring at her and smirking. Then hearing Sherwin telling everyone who'd listen that she was his new girlfriend! Staking some weird public claim to her and then sulking for years because the day after the coffee counter incident made her flee for the back room, begging nice Mrs. Lawson to go up front and work for her until the Evers pair had finished their coffee, picked up their mail and finally cleared out of the Co-op, she met Wade there.

I wish he'd get married or something, she thinks, though I'd pity the poor woman. He fits the profile of a mail-order foreign bride fellow perhaps, disappointed or baffled by feisty, disobedient Canadian women who have a few down to earth expectations of a partner in the 21st century. She can see Evers importing someone who seems docile, someone impressed by microwaves and satellite dishes, someone used to working long, hard hours, then making tea, fetching snacks, safely contained by English as a second language. Maybe a sturdy blonde Russian or Ukrainian woman from the steppes. Surely no Moscow urbanite would be tempted by the likes of him.

Or he'd go for a petite Filipino bride, someone

used to a close-knit family and Mass every Sunday. I would personally offer an escape route, she thinks, and chauffeur the poor woman to the Big Butte airport. I'll bet money that Evers goes into town for sexual relief… oh, ugh! Don't go there, Penny, it's none of your business, it's his business, just get to work.

"He wants this land of ours, always has, just like his Daddy before him," Wade had said and then he'd told her the Toland-Evers saga just before they married. "Matter of fact, his Grand-Daddy tried to have Grandpa's homestead rights cancelled when Gramps went off to the city for an operation or a rest cure, something to do with his head. His nerves were bad, shell shock they called it back then. Anyway, he was laid up for a long time right after World War I and Grandma Amelia kept the place going all by herself, with two kids at the time. You would have liked her, very tough old gal. But one day, she caught Old Evers red-handed, taking parts off our horse-drawn grain drill, which you fill with a few bushels of wheat or oats and then you seed with it. Grandma hauled out the shotgun, the same one we have here now.

"The old thief tried to justify himself at first, telling her she wouldn't be putting a crop in anyway, not with her husband off dying and not likely to make it back. That did it. She fired once over his head and then levelled it at his chest, telling him to drop every washer, bolt and piece of metal he'd taken off our seed drill. He started to talk his way out of it, which was a big mistake, and she let fly somewhere to the left of him. He scrabbled at his pockets and started hurling stolen stuff at the ground any which way. Bigger mistake. She fired another load to the right of him and he pissed his pants and turned and ran, tossing metal parts for a few more strides. Boy, did they all hate each other after that!

"Grandma Amelia put in the crop that spring too, every bit as handy with horses and farm equipment as a man. Grandpa was a bit strange though, to tell you the truth, wandering aimlessly around the place, like he was in a different world. Sometimes we'd find him hiding, not answering when we called him for supper. Other times he'd go to bed for a couple of weeks and we could hear him yelling up there. He had horrible nightmares. All that war stuff coming back to haunt him.

"Then he'd get up one day and be out on the land working like a demon and she'd practically have to haul him off the fields so he'd eat properly. He'd try to make up for the time he'd lost to being sick but he would never talk about it with anyone except Grandma. She had endless patience and kindness under that tough outer layer.

"The land saga continued with the next generation. Old Evers' son Melvin, whom we called Young Evers, Sherwin's proud papa, tried to cancel Morris' lease on the breaks when it was still Crown land for grazing purposes. Clomped into the government agent's office with some trumped-up queries about what was going on with that land because it didn't look like there were enough head of stock being grazed on it by those Tolands to qualify them for a grazing permit. We'd always suspected that Evers bunch of slithering under our fence to inspect our cattle and horses, counting how many calves there were, calculating our income per pound come fall and so on. This episode just confirmed it.

"But none of their plots ever worked because the government agents would take one look at a bushy-headed male Evers specimen licking its liver-like lips, standing at their counter fondling a map of the township, and hustle him out of that office as fast as possible.

"Who knows what new schemes are whirling round and round in that big, shaggy head of Sherwin's? It's inbred, you know, sort of a genetic trait, for an Evers to covet whatever we Tolands have down here. They won't stir themselves to work off their land either because it's beneath them to work for or with anyone else, even the kind of short and long haul trucking I do for the apiaries and fescue growers now. It's a sign of failure to them, working off the land, earning anything except by full-time farming in any respect. So they'll live on spuds and turnips and out-of-season deer and call themselves real farmers. Which qualifies them as real men in their eyes only, I'd guess."

Penny had said, "Well, if times get really tough, you can swagger on up there and say 'I'll throw in the wife and the new hay-baler and we'll work out a land swap.'" Very snappy, so sure of herself, so sure of them both. That had cracked Wade up.

Penny makes her tea from dried leaves she'd harvested from the spearmint patch in August and she tries to think how long it's been since she and Wade had really laughed about something like that. Sometime in the spring, surely, before all this debt business came out into the open and blighted their lives. But she can't think what it was they might have laughed about then. She sips the good tea and tries not to dwell on things she cannot change. She'd rather watch *Jeopardy* and go to bed early, just to take her mind off her own troubles and to reassure herself that she still has a few answers to a few of life's questions, no matter how far-removed from her own life they will surely be. And the farther, the better.

*   *   *

The island men are waiting when Norman drives the truck off the last of two ferries from Vancouver Island to finally reach this island. Cowichan sweaters and toques, one dark beard, one red beard, driving a new 4x4. After a beckoning wave, they follow the vehicle down narrow, twisty roads overhung with dark cedars, in a relentless downpour of rain. The rain makes opening the windows for fresh air out of the question and so they both sit silently, smelling their own and each other's rank sweat. Fatigue has well and truly set into Wade's bones and his back aches miserably. He's been popping eye-drops and drinking water steadily on this trip, trying to combat his bleary state.

They are shown to a small cottage that smells a little of mildew. Norman says the accommodations are all part of the deal with these new buyers; it has to be this way because there is no ferry off this particular island tonight. They'd leave after loading and unloading in the morning.

"That fine with you, Wade?"

Wade nods. Something about the tone of Norman's voice sounds an odd note to him, like he's being told to back off or something. He doesn't want to get into hassling about details with Norman or to come across as controlling and overbearing just because it is the first time Norman has arranged all the buyers. In June, Wade had handed the regular list over to him, given him the phone numbers, all of it, because he had too much going on with Morris dying, then the short haul trucking season of grain, up at 4 a.m. most days, the early barley, then the oats, and finally the wheat harvest kicking in, twelve to fourteen hours a day for nearly sixty days straight. He'd taken time off for Morris' funeral on July 28th but Penny had arranged it all and made all their appointments for the legalities and the grim bank business.

Norman 'had it all under control' and 'the whole shebang of honey pre-sold', so Wade didn't fuss and was just grateful it was taken care of. But with this long haul for the apiaries, apparently, their Island Co-op buyer had bowed out of the sale, after years of Wade hauling their barrels of clover, alfalfa and fire-weed honey down to him. Norman rescued them all by scouting out this new business, so Wade isn't going to act like a bossy foreman and start barking at him now. Norman has even lined up some return freight so they won't have to deadhead all the way home.

Wade kicks off his boots and packs his bag over to the cot, grimacing as his damp, sweaty socks leave faint tracks on the floor tiles behind him. Sighing with relief, he yanks them off and pulls on a pair of clean, thick socks.

Norman pokes around and produces several cans of cold beer from the fridge. Wade puts a nice stash of cedar kindling, old newspaper and a few pieces of dry driftwood into the small wood heater and gets the fire roaring in minutes.

They'd had a bowl of good clam chowder many hours ago on the first ferry from the mainland to Vancouver Island, but here there is a big basket of goodies on the table for them. Very thoughtful. They certainly have gone the extra mile to be hospitable, Wade thinks. All kinds of plums and grapes and three different cheeses and smoked salmon and warm sourdough bread and chewy, gooey brownies. They demolish the food and two more beers and then Wade sinks like a stone on his cot beside the heater. Norman leaves for the truck because he says he is partial to the firm mattress in the sleeper.

When Wade wakes, his head feels like a dry pumpkin with too few seeds inside. But Norman has the coffee made and is whistling something cheerful from "La Boheme". The wood fire is crackling away and the place smells wonderful. The stench of dank mildew has been replaced with cedar wood and coffee and the aromas of another feast laid out for them.

"We got Len over there in Duncan to thank for this business," says Norman, spooning gobs of homemade apple and blackberry jam onto a steaming scone. "He felt bad about his store management switching to the cheaper U.S. and Mexican honey blends, or was it some Australian and Argentinean blend? More free trade fallout I bet, and he made sure we'd get another buyer down here. These fellas might look like they wouldn't have a lot on the ball but you should see their equipment and vehicles, boats and all! Big dryers and smokehouses for salmon and seaweed and God knows what-all. Pretty impressive operation."

Wade decides to take a stroll around the place since the rain has stopped and Norman says they have five hours to wait for the next ferry. It means driving at night and taking three different ferries again to get back to the Mainland, well after dark, but that's fine with them both. Cooler air, much less traffic and one of them can sleep for a good six hours.

Their cottage is perched on the edge of a cliff and around its edge are more cottages, all with little porches facing the sea, clad in cedar siding and shingled roofs. Straight out of *Hansel and Gretel*, thinks Wade. Funky Hippy Chainsaw Architecture, Norman calls it. A collection of modern, long buildings with green metal roofs lines the bay below the cliffs. Probably the salmon smoking and seaweed drying sheds, he figures.

The tide is out and beyond this shallow bay with four small boats stranded in the tidal mud flats, he can see several heavily treed small islands and an automated light blinking from a menacing outcrop of solid rock. The Pacific Ocean is a dark grey-green all the way to the horizon and the sky is an opalescent grey that masks the sun. Wade squints in the diffuse glare of it all. He remembers his sunglasses are back in the truck but can't be bothered to go back for them.

When he'd asked Norman earlier about unloading the honey, he'd said some of the men and he had done the job already that morning. 'Used a skookum front-end loader too, no handcarts to wrestle those seven hundred pound drums of honey around. All that was left was to load up their smoked salmon for the drop-off in Rock Creek.' He'd waved their cheque at him and winked, not handing it over.

What the hell was that all about? Wade asks himself, again, why didn't he just speak up there and then and say, 'Thanks, Norman. I'll be taking that, seeing as it's my truck and I'll be paying your wages in seven days?' But no, something held him back. And when he'd asked where the ferry schedule had gotten to, Norman just laughed and said they'd get off the island in good time, 'a day to rest up from the long drive wasn't going to be a serious delay, was it, Mister Time-keeper?'

Wade tries to act nonchalant about the tone of that comment and keeps looking for the schedule, without being obvious about it. Steering this beast in rush hour traffic isn't his idea of a good time. Even though Norman usually does the driving through the cities, he gets all nervous and frantic too, cursing at the bad drivers and red lights. All his yelling gets Wade on edge, not being a big yelling type himself. When he drives in city traffic, Wade just hangs on tight to the wheel and drives as slowly as he feels necessary, no matter who is flipping their wigs behind him yapping away about a big old International truck in their Type A hyperactive cell-phone. The more nervous he gets, the slower he drives until he gets so slow a new tractor could outpace him.

Norman comes from New York City so maybe yelling is in his blood. But he's been living in Canada for just over thirty years so Wade thinks, and not for the first time, that some basic, quiet politeness must have rubbed off on him by now. Wade doesn't know all that much about New York other than reading mysteries set in the city. And watching David Letterman whenever he gets home close to midnight, wired with coffee and needing to settle down before going to bed where Penny has been asleep since 9:30 p.m. Norman doesn't quite fit in to all of that witty New York set somehow. He is more like a character from a hardboiled detective novel, someone with a favourite Irish pub, connections on the street, a rough and ready kind of guy. Still, for all his rough ways and the fact that Penny doesn't like him though she doesn't come right out and say so, in so many words, he thinks Norman is a good driver and someone different, a change, for company on the road. That's all that counts in the end, good driving and reasonably cheerful company.

Wade walks downhill on the blackberry-bordered path, pausing to eat a few late berries, until he comes to a clearing with a bright blue cottage. The rainbow-shaped sign announces 'Sea-Shore Play School' and he notices some children beside a sandbox have stopped playing and are staring at him. He smiles and waves at them and they all keep staring at him, except for one small shaggy blond boy who gives him the middle finger and then turns around and bares his tiny, pale buttocks at him. Several tykes roar at this display but the rest melt away into the salal and giant ferns. Wade tries not to show his puzzlement or whatever his true feelings are, his disappointment or even sadness. He keeps walking, pretending he hasn't noticed, and hasn't wondered where the boy learned that kind of stuff. He keeps his head down, watching out for thick roots and thorny brambles snaking across the path.

Which is a good thing because two little boys, one about six years of age and the other around four or so, are squatting in the middle of the damp trail. Wade towers over them, looking down at whatever it is the two boys, still unaware of him, are intent on examining. There an earthworm writhes, covered in ants while the little boys watch.

"Excuse me," Wade says and stretches his long legs over the entire collection: boys, earthworm, ants. Then he turns around, bends, and scoops the earthworm up, blowing and flicking the ants off it. He gently places the worm off to one side of the path.

"It's hurting that worm, which is a good kind of worm for the ground, when those mean little ants bite it," he says to the open-mouthed boys and he turns away from them quickly in case they, too, disappoint him with profanities and bare asses. But they remain silent and he's relieved.

The path downhill to the bay turns into a long zig-zag flight of wooden stairs anchored to the cliffs. He is wearing his driving boots, his cowboy boots. The stairway looks like three hundred steps at least. Suddenly he doesn't want to inspect whatever operation they have going down there. There has to be a roadway to get to it and that reminds him that he wants to hit the road and not hang around here any longer than necessary. He will have a firm but friendly chat with Norman on this matter. He heads back up the long trail to the guest cottage. All the children are out of sight and again, he is relieved not to have to encounter them. Where are the adults anyway? Other than the two men who'd guided them here last night, Bodhi and Rafael, he has yet to see a grown-up person.

Norman isn't at the cottage. Wade doesn't feel like

searching the whole property for him so he decides to take a long overdue shower. He realizes his back feels just fine too as the oversized deluxe showerhead pulsates along his spine with steaming needles of hot water. It feels wonderful and so does the huge, luxurious bath towel. He pulls on a clean change of clothes from his duffel bag, shoving his old stuff into the plastic laundry bag to trap the odour of socks and body sweat. Then he finds an up-to-date ferry schedule tucked in amongst the Gardens West and Pacific Yachting magazines in the wicker basket beside the toilet. He can finally relax. Three more hours to go.

He feels new hunger pangs and quickly downs a couple of the freshly made, chewy chocolate brownies and a big bowl of fresh fruit salad which must have been put on the table while he was in the shower, along with more hot coffee. Everything tastes so good and smells so fine and the land and sea breezes nip around his nose, cedar and salt and iodine, as he stands there in the doorway of the cottage. A big arbutus tree shades the porch and Wade spends some time studying the peeling red scrolls of bark and the thick leathery leaves and then he sits down to study all of it again. Everything on the west coast is so exotic and lush and abundant. Wade marvels, inhaling the salt air.

A pair of bald eagles chitter away at each other. If he squints and shades his eyes from the bright shards of the late afternoon sun, he can see them, up high in the Douglas fir branches beside the cottage. He hears the wind flitting through the needles of the fir and he wishes he could understand the eagles. Their high anxious voices are such a contrast to their fierce-eyed photographs and their ancient reputations as the king of the birds. Wade leans back to watch them and wishes, not for the first time, that he could fly too, unassisted by mechanical, manmade constructions. He ponders his earthbound predicament for a good while longer, unable to move.

Norman wanders back to the cottage, carrying a large platter of food. Wade has completely settled in to one of the porch Adirondack chairs, clean and full and relaxed. The sun has broken through completely, banishing the oppressive grey cloud cover. The day is suddenly and gloriously blue, splashed with every shade of green and peeling arbutus red.

Wade thinks he needs to ask Norman something and says so. They both wait a while for the question to emerge but it doesn't emerge and Wade apologizes, three times.

Norman kindly interrupts, "It'll come along, just give it time."

Meanwhile, he pats down all his pockets and retrieves the honey cheque, saying, "Hey, man, meant to do this earlier but you took off. By the way, those salmon packs are all loaded and we're ready to go."

All is well between them, just like old times, good buddies. Then he starts with the jokes.

"The chicken and the egg were laying in bed."

Wade snickers. Norman wrinkles his forehead.

"Not yet, not yet. Oh, okay, I getcha. Okay. Mister Chicken is smoking a good cigar and looking up at the ceiling with a little smile on his beak. Little Egg looks straight ahead, a real blank look, and she says 'Well, *now* I guess we both know the answer to *that* question.'"

And Wade smiles, then laughs his head off, sitting out on that little porch overlooking the sea, drinking the excellent, dark roast coffee, sinking his teeth into the best brownies in the whole, wide world.

Norman opens the fridge and roars something about when in Rome, selecting a dark oatmeal brew for himself and handing Wade his requested amber ale from the assortment of micro-brewery beers on the shelves. He also whips the tea towel off the platter he's brought over, heaped high with smoked, peppered salmon chunks and teriyaki-smoked and Cajun-smoked salmon as well as Indian candied salmon and a round loaf of fresh sourdough bread. They fall on it, building immense sandwiches, adding capers and dried black olives, slathering them with tarragon mayonnaise and fresh lemon squeezed quickly over the lot.

"Never look a gift horse in the yap, et cetera," Norman sighs and belches happily, shoving the platter aside at last and taking a swig from his second beer, a hemp cream ale which he pronounces mighty tasty.

And Wade laughs and laughs and falls asleep there on the porch.

*　　　　*　　　　*

When I woke up, it was dark and raining. Norman was gone. I felt a little queasy and stiff and dry-mouthed but I made himself go and look for Norman after drinking at least four glasses of fine-tasting well water. There were paths leading in several directions but I thought I could hear laughing and music so I followed my ears.

What happened next is still a strange sort of blur to me. They were dancing in a hall, a long building with a little stage at one end. There were children dancing in rings, the most beautiful children, all different colours. And other circles of women—young, willowy, beautiful women and older, curvy, sexy women with laughing eyes. Knowing eyes. I remember thinking of Penny, at which point I quit ogling like a hick even though I'd never seen so many beautiful women all in one place before. I think it's safe to say this place is probably some kind of hippie co-op, some second-generation commune or ashram and alternative school operation maybe.

Norman surprised the hell out of me by jumping in the middle of one of their circles and doing a wacky little dance. The women all laughed and swooped around him, encouraging the silly fool.

I was really hungry so I ate more food from the long table there and drank a killer punch. Homemade mead, someone said, as a kind of thank you to us. The men all nodded and smiled and said how excellent our honey was. Norman was being pursued by a red-haired Viking woman who towered over him by a good six inches.

Now I don't dance much at the best of times but there I was, hoofing around with these lovelies, not even feeling ridiculous about the way I dance in clumsy, jerky spasms. Everybody else was cutting the rug any which way they pleased and having themselves a fine old time.

"What the hay, we'll leave first thing tomorrow morning," I said to Norman as he went jigging by near the front of a long conga line I'd just joined too. Bright-eyed, bushy-faced men were playing drums and guitars and singing tunes I didn't quite recognize. Maybe it's because I'm clean-shaven and about six-two in my cow-boy boots, but I couldn't help noticing almost all the men were short, bearded guys wearing baggy, bright clothes except for a couple of other skinny beanpoles like me. The women were all wearing those flowing hippie dresses, no jeans or plaid flannel shirts in sight.

Not like my Penny. She wears a dress twice a year maybe, to weddings and funerals. Has her white blouse and black skirt for her choir concerts but except for those, she lives in her old jeans and flannel shirts or puts on one of her starchy teacher pantsuits. Blue, green or brown. She looks good, you know, she's always had a trim little figure, curvy in all the right spots, don't get me wrong but she will spend money on horse tack sooner than on herself. And thrifty is her middle name. She mends all our clothes and darns our socks. All that sort of thing.

So I moved around the edge of the packed dance hall, getting my bearings, glad I had their honey cheque, thinking how I had to send it to Penny first thing when we got to the Mainland. Thinking how I should surprise her with a swoopy dress with lots of purple in it, something filmy and flirty for her little gymnast kind of body, nothing that she would ever buy because it might go out of style too fast and she couldn't wear it for eight years straight. I'd have to tell her I got it on sale so she could relax enough to enjoy it.

Norman was having a great time, dancing with the tall Viking, grinning like a madman. I stepped outside for a breather and a little clump of people on the porch offered me a joint.

"What the hay," I said, "it's been years but when in Rome, eh?"

They laughed at that, like it was some original wit on my part, and we stayed out on the porch for a considerable while. I coughed like crazy, never was much of a smoker of any kind, but I chased the weed with some more mead punch and then my spineless body separated from my head.

I found my back up against a porch post, with a black-haired beauty plastered to me, one of the curvy women who'd been in my line of sight most of the evening. The others had gone back inside, I guess. I tried to talk, I think, but she just kept grinning at me, touching the front of my shirt, slipping her fingers past the buttons, onto my skin and then we went at it, necking like teenagers.

She was wearing a floaty sort of dress with not a stitch on underneath. Practically sucked the tongue right outa my head. Whoa boy! Then she jumped up and wrapped both her legs around my waist and leaned back and her breasts, I mean she was really something else, they just sort of spilled out of her dress somehow and I dove right in and just about lost it.

What the hell was I doing there, stoned out of my gourd? I broke away, set her down none too gently, meaning to head for the cottage, not to get in over my stupid, drugged-up head. There's harmless fun and then there's hell to pay, you know? I swear I've never stepped over the traces once in my married life, I swear to God. I've had my chances, on the road you know, and once this silly gal from home, we went to school together, well, she had a mad crush on me for a long while after I married but I wasn't interested in her kind of trouble at all. I haven't thought twice about turning anyone down in that regard.

But this just got going before I knew what I was up to. I'm not used to dope that strong, for starters! She, I don't even know her name, so help me, she pulled me inside the hall for just one more dance.

I remember spinning around the floor and falling, tripping over my own damn cowboy feet, and then being packed off by a bunch of bushy-bearded gnomes. That's all. I was gone, out like a light.

When I woke up, I was in a strange room, in a strange bed. I lay there frozen for a while, hearing somebody else's breathing, thinking oh God, oh God, because I didn't and couldn't remember a thing. Mostly I didn't want to see who it was so I tried to slide out sideways, ever so quietly. I almost made it to the door when a sleepy-soft voice said, 'Hey, we could finish what we started last night, Honey Man.'

I didn't look back. I grabbed my clothes and boots and ran, buck-naked, until I saw a shed I could hide behind to get dressed.

Norman was passed out in the rocking chair at the cottage and took a while to come to, even with me shaking his shoulders good and hard. He wanted to make coffee first but I said no, we had to get moving, that we shouldn't eat or drink a thing. Norman just grinned and reached for a brownie from a fresh basket of goodies on the table.

Fine, I said then, as mad at him as I'd ever been to

that point, you just get stoned for the day but I'm driving us out of here before we're three days late instead of two.

So I drove us down those dark, twisty roads, following the ferry signs I could barely make out in the fog, driving way too fast. We made it onto the ferry with barely a minute to spare before it pulled away. Norman stayed in the truck and snoozed. I walked to the end of the boat, just a small ferry with room for vehicles and not much else, and I stared back at the dock on that island until it disappeared completely in the fog. The ferry blasted its foghorn all the way to the next island for forty minutes. I can still hear that horn now.

You wouldn't even know that island existed from where I stood.

I didn't talk about this with Norman. I worried he might let something slip out at home and that must not ever, I mean it must never, ever happen. I don't know how much he knew, about me and...whoever it was.

I can't ever go back there, I can't deliver anything to that place, ever again. I'm a pretty straight arrow I guess.

Why? I've got too much to lose in the long run. Like I said, Penny, the kids...four generations of To-lands from one small community.... I mean, there'd be such talk. I was no angel when I was, you know, single. Not a real big ladies man but if a young lady was there, willing and all, well, it's part of being young isn't it? All of us farm boys and gals too, all sowing our wild oats, tearing around in our pick-up trucks, going to dances, staying out until dawn, coming home for chores and a full day of work no matter what we'd been up to. Cows had to be milked, hay had to be cut, you worked on two hours of sleep or none at all but you still worked.

No, I'm not bored in that way, no, not really. I mean, a person pretty much settles in after twenty-some years with the same person, you know, it isn't the be-all and end-all like it is when you're just young bloods full of sap, eh? I'd say we both are pretty tired after a day's work and we just want a good night's sleep, especially her... I know it hasn't been all that great lately... for us, not like it used to be...because she's wound up tight about stuff, our troubles.... No, I wouldn't say I'm bored or easily tempted, not that I don't have good eyesight but I've never *acted* on it...not before this and I don't know what-all, don't know what *really* went on there, oh hell, you know I just *can't* remember, it hurts trying...

*   *   *

The call comes for her from Goodland Elementary, a Grade Five class. Two days, maybe three. Perfect timing! Penny has, true to form, worked non-stop at winterizing and cleaning, inside and outside the house. Now, even with the temperature consistently dropping below zero every night, the house feels warmer and smells better.

On the second day of Wade's absence, she washes the walls of the living room with hot water and sudsy ammonia, appalled at the yellowy brown rivulets and the change in the colour of her wash water. Old nicotine, surely. This is confirmed when she puts her nose next to the heavy floral curtains on the one tall window and immediately sneezes four times in a row. Foul! She hauls the stepladder in from the workshop to take them down and puts off the decision to replace them by folding them in a filmy dry-cleaning bag and stuffing them into a cupboard. This motivates her to wash the window in the room and all the others in the house, a three hour job. The outside windows would have to wait for a warm day, which might mean next spring, and the stretch ladder with Wade around to help but she comforts herself with knowing that accumulated grime and odours are banished from the inside.

On the third day, she roto-tills the entire garden under completely except for the bumper crop of pumpkins, which she intends to sell, saving two future grinning sentinels for their own front steps. Even without children at home anymore, she hopes the Dawson and Tupper children will persuade their parents to drive them here. She will make a point of mentioning it to their mothers, in fact. There is still plenty of candy in their freezer from the previous year when only three carloads braved a sleet-filled Hallow-een night to venture as far as the Toland Ranch, the last stop on the valley road.

There's a couple hundred dollars worth, or more, of orange gold out there amongst the blackened vines. Easy to grow too. Maybe next year, she thinks, I'll con-vert more of the patch to pumpkins, do a real job of it. It doesn't pay to grow more potatoes or onions. We can't begin to compete with big growers on the price and we sure can't eat much of them, just the two of us anymore. Wish we could be like some farmers and sell topsoil but we can't spare an inch of it from this land. Wish we could just have some blind good luck for once, grow the right specialty crop in a year when the price was sky high and the growing conditions were perfect, something like that. Which has yet to happen to the likes of us!

Penny heads out at 7:30 a.m. on the fourth day to start the half-hour drive to Goodland Elementary. She is so relieved to have this day and maybe the next two days as well for well-paid subbing work. She hums the last song she heard on the kitchen radio's Golden Moldies program, Kenny Rogers' cheery advice to gamblers. The faithful Dodge Dart will not start. She'd gassed up yesterday while wearing her chore clothes, to avoid stinking up her school clothes and her hands. She taps the battery terminals, stares at the carburetor and the fuel pump, willing them to show something quick and obvious by way of a problem. But the hollow click tells her it's the starter. Flat tires, oil changes, air filter…all that stuff she can fix but the wretched starter is beyond her mechanical abilities.

Penny hates bothering other people for rides, especially when they have to go out of their way but she shoves aside her pride and phones Hazel Collins, her nearest teacher neighbour and Grade Two veteran for nearly thirty years. Pas de problemo, sings Hazel, be glad of good company. Penny takes a deep breath and walks up to the roadside, keeping Casey at arm's length to avoid a swath of black and grey hairs down either side of her blue outfit. Gwyneth and Gordon had both bloomed into fervent readers, soccer players and enthusiastic hand bell ringers thanks to Hazel at the helm of the Good Ship Grade Two year after year.

What a relief. Three days of subbing will cover the next machinery payment. I will give Hazel gas money, she vowed, for the rides to and from the school instead of getting the starter fixed right away.

It's the best she can do for now.

*   *   *

Norman is worth his weight in smoked salmon for trouble-shooting mechanical stuff. It's a good thing too, with the way the old beast always heats up on the Hope-Princeton stretch. Wade just hands him the right wrenches like the head nurse to the surgeon, with the good doctor's head and neck buried in the guts of a 1982 International truck with 312,000 miles on the original engine. So there they are, crippled on the side of the highway at high noon. Despite the fact that it is October 4th, the heat trapped between the high canyon walls is enough to make both of them sweat rivers. The clean smell of sage lingers in the still air and so does the smoke of a recent forest fire, which has left the seared trunks of Ponderosa pines like so many sacrificed knights in a once-mighty army, held upright only by their scaly blackened armour.

"Whazzat?" Norman barks, looking up from his operation on the blown-out radiator hose.

"Not me," says Wade.

"I *know* it's not you, Wade, for Chrissakes! Don't

you hear it? I've got the bum ears here. I can feel something buzzing!"

And then he hears it. A low hum, like hornets over their vandalized grey nest, circling higher and higher, looking for the culprit to sting the life out of, man or beast. Wade looks up into the cloudless sky but there is nothing there, no high jet and no Ultralite craft winging along on its deranged sewing machine motor.

"J.C. Murphy, stay cool," Norman says in a low, tight voice, as they watch them crest the big hill, less than half a klick away. Wade taps him on the leg.

"Are you all done up there? Can we get the hell back on the road?"

"Oh, boyoboy," is all he says. "No, hell, no."

Thirty or forty of them roar toward the truck, chrome flashing in the light. Black sunglasses, black leather suits, silver and black helmets, lots of those ugly little cook-pot helmets, lots of moustaches and beards, and women with sullen, tough mouths. The big guy in front holds up his black gauntlet, and they all swarm to a stop.

Wade sees him grin, all big, gapped yellow teeth. Then he takes off the sunglasses and rubs his one eye. A black patch covers the left eye and his right eye is sunk so deeply in his head, it is impossible to make out the colour or the expression or anything meaningful about it. He weighs close to half a honey barrel, thinks Wade. Just huge. A tiny little woman straddles the back of his big Harley. Albino.

"Freaky," he says, "hop off and say hello to these folks."

She does as he says, taking off her sunglasses quickly

to squint at them with her small pink and ice-blue eyes, pursing her mean little mouth. Wade holds still, his heart thudding away so loudly he can practically hear it hammering under his shirt. He nods at Freaky, thinking how much she looks like a newborn white mouse with no fur, like the ones Gordon raised for pets when he was a kid. She doesn't actually speak, just looks them both over. *Creepy.*

She leans over to the big man and whispers in his ear.

"I'll see about that," he grins even wider, baring his big slab teeth as he slaps her silver leather bum.

Wade doesn't like this. Every bully he's ever known uses that expression. 'I'll see about that!' they'd sneer when they stomped off, making plans to screw up his day. It occurs to him that his father used that expression a lot too, meaning that he would have the final word on the matter, whatever it was. No, Wade doesn't like this at all. Sweat pools from under each armpit and spills down over his ribs.

"So, you gotta problem here?" the big man hollers, looking at Norman. All their motors are still rumbling away and Wade doesn't look at the rest of them, just the big man and his little friend with the icy white face and transparent hair wisping out from under her silver helmet.

"Yeah, radiator hose, but it's okay now. When it cools off enough to do a refill on the rad we'll be fine," yells Norman. Wade can see a sweat line trickling down by Norman's ear and then Norman's paw cuffing at it like it was a tattletale insect.

Meanwhile, Wade has a big urge to pee. For no particular reason, he thinks of Penny and how she'd crack wise about people being so scared you can hear their sphincters slamming shut. He tightens his up. Instantly he feels better and stands straighter, taking a slow, deep breath. It's okay, Penny, he would tell her, I'm gonna stay cool. Everything is gonna be okay. A-okay.

The big man appears not to have heard the mechanical update because he waves another biker with a red handlebar moustache around the other side of the truck and nods at two others who dismount.

"Mind if we have a look?" he asks, as if they have much choice. For one awful moment, Wade thinks they might draw knives and slash through the heavy black tarps on their double-jointed trailer. He remembers the keys and holds them high, shaking them. Freaky snags them in a flash and does her weird little boneless walk to the back of the truck, handing them over to the other pair of thugs. One leaps up and riffles through the keys, very quickly finding the one that unlocked the padlock at the back-end.

That load is going to be a very big disappointment to them. Wade almost laughs, but stifles it in time. Ha-haha bozos.

A white van load of pilgrims drives by slowly, all their pale noses pressed against the windows. First Evangelical Church of the Covenant, Abbotsford, B.C. Big guffaws from the assembled. Wade sees all the heads in the van snap back to face forward. More guffaws. He prays that the pilgrims spotted the name on the side of the truck door and will figure out that Wide Sky Trucking, Goodland, B.C., is not likely to be linked to this roving band of mercenaries. He silently wills them to phone the RCMP in Princeton within the next fifteen minutes. He can see how they'd pray for themselves not to be pursued but he'd very much like them to take the next logical step on Norman's and his behalf too.

"Yup!"

The shout comes from the back of the truck. A grinning biker waves at the big man with the eye patch and swings off with his pal, who locks up, tossing the keys to Freaky again.

"You-all will be escorted to your delivery," hollers the big man, "service, eh?"

Wade guesses he is laughing because his jaw is moving up and down. With all the bike motors revving up again, he can't hear a thing. He wishes he had sprung for a CB in the truck which he'd wanted years ago or a cell-phone now in the 21st century but Penny had vetoed it, didn't want to spend their scarce money on a mere part-time toy. He walks over to the big man and plays it straight.

"We're contracted to deliver honey and salmon to the Dry Belt Potato Producers and to pick up seven tons of Yukon Gold potatoes," he shouts, looking into the small, charcoal-coloured eye. Wade can smell hot metal, hot leather and supremely rotten breath.

"That's us!" the biker shouts back and Wade leans away from the foul wafts. "Get the truck on the road and we'll see you right to the door, fellas. You're a couple days late, you know."

He holds up his gauntlet and the bikes rev to a deafening pitch before moving away, leaving a haze of pale, blue smoke in the air.

"I'll be damned," says Wade. "Those are the customers?"

"Apparently so. Long as their cheque is good, wouldn't you say?"

And this retort from Norman reminds Wade to put the cheque from the Lotus Island people into the envelope and to get it into the first post office he sees after leaving this hell-hole. While Norman fills the radiator from plastic jugs filled with distilled water, Wade finds the stamped envelope and puts the cheque inside, the whole time wishing he could write something upbeat, but coming up dry. So he carefully prints XOXO and S.W.A.K. on the envelope where a return address would normally be written. He leaves it unsealed, thinking of the cheque forthcoming from this unlikely bunch they've just encountered.

Normal is not the name of the game on this trip, little gal, and that isn't the half of it. Hang on, he wants to tell her, I'm just about halfway home.

*   *   *

It's strange Wade hasn't called yet but no news is good news. Penny consoles herself several more times during the morning. She'd repeated that self-same sentence to Hazel on the drive into school yesterday. Everything's okay, A-okay. Really.

Today she's glad it's Saturday, glad for this crisp, clear fall day to burn up the yard trash, glad for three days of teaching under her belt already. The annual autumnal exchange of back to school colds between students and teachers is well underway and she almost feels guilty about her gratefulness for the predictability of weakened immune systems. But no, she won't indulge in that. She rarely suffers a cold anymore, a consequence, she believes, of ingesting her homemade rose-hip tea and lots of berries, garlic and vegetables in her diet. And the overriding fact, she admits, is that Gwyneth and Gordon weren't bringing nasty little microbes home from school either; like snotty-nosed gifts for their own parents.

She is glad for the work and, unlike the tender souls who shudder at the thought of being a substitute teacher, Penny is secure about being one of the good ones, with plenty of diversions to counteract ninety-nine percent of the stunts she encounters in the classrooms. Besides, she knows nearly all the kids and they know her. And they know that she knows all their parents. It would be different in town, she is well aware, and she is glad she doesn't have to cope with the legendary bad behaviour of town kids.

Adding to her gratitude for the world at large, Penny mentally lobs another fervent thank you to Hazel's son, Sean, for agreeing to rebuild the starter on the mighty Dodge Dart and for scrounging four barely used high-end winter tires from the garage he worked at. He is trading the tires and his work for their Dodge Fargo truck which has been rusting away in the weeds for twenty odd years. He's thrilled. Penny's thrilled too, especially because he doesn't really want it for himself after all. He just wants it for an interesting restoration project and she's got first dibs on buying it back. It could be a surprise twenty-fifth anniversary present for Wade next June if she can somehow sell something for two thousand dollars, like Maggie-May, except she doesn't ever want to sell her favourite horse.

Penny hauls the wheelbarrow out of the garage and heads for the pumpkin patch. It might be a good idea to have some dry and ready to go pumpkins, she thinks, and then she stops, remembering she has to wait until Sean fixes the car starter. But he'd said he could probably have it ready for her by Monday afternoon, so she can still pick the ones that are nicely orange already and store them in the garage until the Farmer's Market Harvest Sale next Saturday. The weather is supposed to turn tomorrow and if they are in for a wet spell, she doesn't look forward to trundling a wheelbarrow loaded with pumpkins out of the mud or worse, having them rot on the ground.

If Maggie-May would only produce a foal next spring from Mister Bojangles, then maybe she could train it and sell something very fine. But Maggie-May's not an easy catcher and she's had just one foal, born dead. Mr. Bojangles might be fifteen years old or he might be twenty, and he might be prone to lameness but Penny's still glad she rescued him from the dog-food buyer this spring. As long as his male equipment is in working order, she mutters to herself, I can help him cope with arthritis and I'm still not one hundred percent convinced that the arthritis diagnosis is accurate either. He seemed very springy of step the other day when I walked out to see the gang on the old brome field pasture. Maybe his former home in a tiny corral with sloppy wet manure and mud up to his fetlocks most of the time is the real reason for his prolonged stiffness.

She hopes his papers are to be believed and will pay off for years to come but she needs good-looking proof on four legs before standing him at stud and charging for any service. Mister Bojangles deserves to retire gracefully with quality mares in attendance, nice dry winter quarters with clean straw underfoot and prime alfalfa hay and chopped oats in the manger. Warm bran mash if he wants it, on those really cold thirty below days.

She puts on her work gloves to handle the prickly pumpkin vines and starts loading the wheelbarrow, carefully distributing the future jack o' lanterns. Yes, a little Doc Bar Quarterhorse and Standard Bred-cross filly or colt with Maggie-May would be just dandy, she thinks, and if he throws good-looking sons and daughters with everyone else's mares, well, so much the better.

Word would get around. The wealth from the oil and gas industry had spawned hobby farms around the towns in the region and those big homes on quarter-sections or the dodgy deals with politicians for small acreages on prime farm land always had white rail fences around their pastures and a few leggy blood-horses grazing there. Hobby horses, pampered pets, not hard-ridden rodeo stock or guide and outfitter pack-horses. She doesn't want to raise her horses to such hard-working vocations. Hers would be pleasure horses, fine companions with gentle mouths and excellent manners and beautiful gaits. Riding one at a lope would be like sitting on a floating rocking chair.

On Monday, she plans to call up the people who owe them trucking money if she doesn't find their cheques in the mailbox. There are only three more days until the next payment comes due and the School

Board cheque for her October subbing won't get to her until November 9th, if she's lucky. On Monday evening, she will be able to show up for the first choir practice of the season at St. Matilda's. If the car is fixed like Sean promised and if he doesn't find some other fresh hell under the hood…

The clanging outdoor ring of the phone interrupts her silent planning session. She carefully sets down her loaded wheelbarrow and sprints to the workshop.

Wade! Let this be good news, please! Let me not forget to tell you I always miss you by the end of the first week alone, without fail every trip, and love. Yes, 'I love you' and 'take care' and 'drive home safely'. I'll say them all out loud like I should have done when you left.

The line hums.

"Hello?"

Nothing. She strains to listen.

"Hello?"

"Well, hello there, Penny. Sherwin here, Sherwin Evers? How are you today?"

"Fine!" she snaps, utterly disappointed. "What's up?"

"Well, that new stud of yours, that cottontail chestnut fella, I noticed him standing with one foot up, in the first field after the bridge. Noticed him off by himself there yesterday too."

"Oh? Well, I'll check it out. Okay then. Thanks for calling about it today. Bye."

"Do you need a hand?"

"No. Thanks for letting me know, today."

Penny smacks the phone down. Why didn't you

call me yesterday if you saw a horse with his foot dangling, you fuzzy-headed dolt?! How can he get to water like that? Give me a hand, my foot! I'll whistle up Casey and grab a halter. It's a good half-hour walk to that pasture. Hell and damn! Wait, I'd better take some oats and water for him. Better yet, take the pick-up. He's still a little shy, hanging back while the others get all the treats and attention first. Doesn't do the alpha male thing yet with this bossy bunch of young mares, my gentle old boy.

But a vet bill for him is not what I want to deal with right now. Money, money, bloody money!

She doesn't understand why Wade runs away to drive that damn truck, leaving this place for a bad case of eyestrain, a sore back, greasy spoons with that braying ass of a bully he drives with. I know it's decent money, trucking, she admits, it's kept us going for all these years so I'll never complain out loud. I just wish he'd come up with something he could do here on the ranch that would pay reliably and that wouldn't keep him away from home so much.

But I'll never, ever tell him how it bothers me to see his face so lit up and happy as he's heading out our door. Or how fed up I am with the way he jumps my bones within half a minute of getting home, no matter what I'm doing or how I'm feeling. He's just gotta drop his load. Horny as a hop-toad.

God, I feel so old and weary just thinking about us that way. We used to be so great in that department. I'd never have believed we'd ever get like this. All the joy of it crushed by money worries, exactly as predicted by those gee whiz quizzes in women's magazines. She has to admit that she is just gut-kicked by this turn in their lives.

What else to do? What else to sell? The chop mill to Evers? Not unless I get the go-ahead from Wade and then I'd have to argue against it. It's better to chop oats for horses like Mister Bojangles with inefficient teeth. The fall steers are gone and the money's been spent on the fuel bill, dorm fees, and overdue taxes. There's still more incoming bills from Morris and the estate muddle.

If Gwyneth and Gordon didn't manage to win scholarships and qualify for student loans and work hard at their summer jobs, they'd be sunk. Penny knows this. The cost of their books alone is what I used to pay for a whole year's tuition.

Horses, well, there's always them. Don't buy anything that eats while you sleep, Morris said to her, every chance he got. It took years before he allowed them to board horses out here on the breaks and on the mowed hay fields. Perfect sideline for an operation like this. Typical Morris. Got kicked by a horse he was bashing around when he was a young bully and he'd never liked one after that. A case of mutual disrespect. She always took his pearls of wisdom with a block of salt.

Oh please, Mister Bojangles, please let this be a simple barb wire cut, not a break or a sprain. I need to get you home, to water and food, get you away from that young stud I'm boarding, against my better judgment, who will soon figure out you can't fight back if he's feeling frisky. Then there'll be a shuffle in the pecking order once the alpha horse is out of commission.

No, stop worrying about the young guy, she thinks. He's not even two years old yet. Stop worrying.

Land. We could sell some of the land.

No.

It's barely enough to support us now, she admits, and we're leaving it to both the kids. Gordon might even want to set up his vet practice right here and Gwyneth, well, she could do what she liked with her half. She loves it too. Maybe she'll even teach here, in Goodland, with at least three-quarters of the staff well over forty-five years old right now. We'd buck the trend, she's told Wade, having our kids come home to the ranch and even be able to work here! So many others will never come back. So many families are moving, selling out, leaving for town jobs or retiring in the Okanagan or on Vancouver Island to manage apartments or something, anything that pays them a living wage and keeps a roof over their heads. Who can blame them?

If Wade cared more about the place, and if Morris hadn't controlled everything, he might have found something better to grow here, something specialized, something that paid well for once, that wasn't as much work as hay, that wasn't so dependent on this risky weather or the speculators in pork belly futures and whatnot. Add to this global cattle diseases and quarantines and Argentinean beef dumping, U.S. fruit dumping and more stupid, short-sighted plans to flood even more priceless Peace River valley land with another short-lived, silt-laden dam at Site C. And it's a wonder people still have the heart and mind, never mind the fully functioning aging bodies, to get up every morning to farm and ranch.

But she knows it's not Wade's fault.

Don't go blaming him, she has to remind herself. Morris didn't give him an inch of slack. Or let him contribute any ideas. Wade gave up on farming ideas years ago. Just drove truck for the apiaries and everyone else until he could buy his own. No wonder he jumps at the chance to get out of here as often as he can.

She tells herself that she knows as much about the place as Wade does. Hell, I was Morris' ranch hand just as much as Wade ever was and I looked after the garden and all the food harvesting for both houses as well.

We can't sell this place now. We stayed put instead of moving away and starting a new life somewhere. Somewhere Wade might have become something more, she thinks for the umpteenth time. He might have finished more than one year of college. Who knows what he might have found out about himself? But we just stayed put, holding on to the land and for what? To pass it on. Well, the wheel goes round and round doesn't it?

Casey prances in front of her, grinning, his shiny coat so thickened up for winter that he looks every bit the burly Yukon dog he is.

I could have held onto a teaching job if Morris hadn't been running Wade ragged seven days a week and telling us how lucky we were to have free rent. Wade could have looked after the kids more often and I might have worked at a permanent part-time position. I'd have a half-decent pension, half-decent benefits and lots of holidays…oh, what's the use! That's what a sensible person would have done.

Stay positive. Count your blessings. Don't let things get to you. Hang on! These are the little motivational talks she is constantly preaching. Look at this place! Growing and selling good quality hay, raising and boarding horses, having bees on the land for a share of the honey, keeping two hundred purebred Angus cattle, a dozen chickens, a few pigs and a huge garden the two of them don't need anymore and that she can barely keep up with harvesting...and here they are, struggling even harder to make a living, and a way, way deeper in debt than when they started out twenty-four years ago.

God, if you're around, please, we need a break.

*   *   *

They are, so far as he can tell, in a camp of about sixty people, most of them living in trailers and old school buses except for the Quebecois who have teepees a ways off from the others in the trees. Psycho lives in a giant log lean-to which is actually part of the front entrance to the storage caves for the potatoes. Amazing set-up, using old mine-shafts to store spuds at a perfectly cool temperature year round, with a working tram-line to haul them down and back up again.

They have handcarts and enough muscle-bound types to wrestle the loads on and off, without either Wade or Norman to help. Their second-in-command, Red Handlebar Moustache, had just waved his dismissive meaty paw when they pointed out their compact hydraulic forklift behind the sleeper.

They peel back the heavy tarp and unload the honey and salmon and swiftly load the spuds like they've been doing it all their lives. Their display of swaggering competence is a surprising comfort to Wade so he and Norman just stand around and nod wisely, accepting the cool cans of beer that Psycho and Freaky offer them.

Wade sips carefully at his beer, refusing a second one, figuring he'll drive out just as soon as they're done with the loading. The beer is stored down in the mine shaft too. What a set-up, he marvels again, thinking about the old root-cellar dug into the small hill behind the house on the ranch. They used it for potatoes but only as a temporary measure if the weather turned to rain or a quantity sale was in the offing because mice quickly found ways to infiltrate. He thinks about the ancient wooden door his Grandpa Gavin had built for it and how he needs to make a new one.

There is now one-third of the load of honey left and half the smoked salmon, for two more deliveries. The front trailer is completely filled with bagged potatoes for the north. Wade has their cheque in the envelope safely tucked in his button-down shirt pocket. It is already nearly dark, cooling down nicely, and he reckons he can drive east and make the Kootenays by morning if they just leave now. The past few hours with Norman at the wheel and the bikers in front of them managed to spoil one of his favourite drives along the pretty Similkameen River, past the mounds of pumpkins and squash outside the fruit stands of tidy Keremeos, the organic orchards of Cawston and the gleaming white hotels of Osoyoos with its highway-side fruit stands and yet more orchards and vineyards bordering Osoyoos Lake. Even crawling up Anarchist Mountain, a half hour gear-crunching marathon was more gruelling than usual, just knowing this bunch was waiting for them in the shade of the rest-stop at the summit.

"Norman, my man!" roars Psycho, clapping a hairy paw on Norman's back.

Psycho seems to have taken a shine to Norman. Norman stumbles a little but manages a hearty-looking grin.

"Stay for the Q, why doncha, you 'n 'Wade here?"

"Yeah, why not?" says the worthless side-kick. Wade still hasn't gotten over the highway rendezvous with this gang of so-called spud farmers and he does not want to hang around socializing with them either. But Red Handlebar bellows and grabs them both around the shoulders, propelling them toward the bonfires and the barbeque.

Wade stumbles over a thick tree root across the path. He keeps his eyes downcast and rages in silence. For the past six years, he's dropped honey barrels off to the straight arrows at the Vancouver Island Federated Co-op, then delivered to the even straighter arrows at the South Okanagan Interior Co-op, and finished up with a scenic drive on the Highway 3 route to the orchards of Creston before heading back north on the Thompson highway to home again. None of the Co-ops are involved on this trip, so far, which is very odd. And yet Norman has done a good job getting set up with these new buyers. They won't be dead-heading a cubic centimetre of space at this rate either, what with all the salmon and spuds, and the usual apples due up ahead in Creston.

As well, his food budget isn't suffering, thanks to the hospitality on the road this time. He hasn't touched much of the dry goods, the rye crispbreads and stoned wheat thin crackers or the cheese and smoked ham Penny packed for him. She would be glad of this but she wouldn't be crazy about the company he's been keeping, free vittles or not.

The evening air is already filled with the aromas of barbecued beef and the loud and distorted clashings of some thrash metal band. Norman smirks and whispers anthrax or white snake or something into Wade's ear but Wade turns away, steps away from him before he punches his lights out. Not that he's sure he can. Norman's built like a solid brick outhouse even though he doesn't reach Wade's shoulders in height.

He lets Red Handlebar and Norman step ahead of him on the path and then just stops, watching their broad backs recede into the tricky, fading light.

Why can't I just speak up, Wade wonders, say we're hitting the road now, Jack, and that's all there's to it? He is pushing his luck on this trip. Maybe this really is the last ride with old Norman if his attitude is going to be like this. It doesn't sit well with me and just because he did me a favour by organizing the drops for the cargo this once because of Morris dying and me run ragged all summer, it doesn't mean he gets to strut around like he's in charge, as if this was his business and his truck. The Co-ops didn't warn me they were unhappy enough to switch suppliers and bring in all this blended international honey, but what do I know? I'm just the delivery guy. I just don't think they'd be allowed to switch to some cheap honey blend when we produce so much of it here in this province. I don't think the Co-op boards would allow something like that. It would ruffle too many nationalist farmer feathers and be just plain wrong-headed. Bad business decisions all around. He decides he's going to check into that story when he gets back.

Truth is, and he knows it's the truth as he stands and pees into the pine needles in the gathering dusk, he's afraid of this gang of bikers. Where are the fields, for starters? If they're potato farmers, he's a Formula One racer. Or a figure-skating champion. The junior female one.

He isn't sleepy and he isn't hungry either so he doubles back to the truck, unlocks the door and climbs into the sleeper to read. He keeps his books in the glovebox, so that he always has one on hand to read during the line-ups at the elevators or to coast through the usual sorts of loading delays on the farms. Or for times like now when he is trapped with no place to hang out but inside his truck. He sighs as he stretches out on the bed. It always feels good to get horizontal too, to flatten right out and give his tensed-up back a rest.

His travel book-light lights up the pages just perfectly, so he closes the sleeper curtains and feels that private, peaceful feeling he craves after a day like he's had. He sinks into *Lightning*, a fictional history of the West, and the story of Doc, a soft-hearted, hardheaded man he hopes will survive the psychopath on his trail. He especially loves the way the horses are described, how important they are to the men, and the way young-old Doc is like a father to the drifting younger cowboys who are not yet whole grown men. Not that Doc is yet either, not quite, but at least he is aware of what a good man can be like, no thanks to his own father, all credit going to his good uncle, hanged by vigilantes who may have been Masons in a mountain mining town. Lots to consider, many layers of social and personal stuff, a good "guy" book, as the nice fellow in the Big Butte Bookstore described it when Wade sauntered in for his monthly stack of new and used books. He knows Wade's tastes and hasn't put a foot wrong yet.

He would have to pass this one on to Penny, for sure, with the horse-human bond in mind. She reads much more slowly than he does, claiming not to have as much time to read as him because she spends her extra hours either sewing or editing the articles for the Goodland history book, all true. She goes to her choir practices every Monday evening from October to the middle of May as well.

He loves reading. It keeps his brain alive and connected to the world out there, keeps his imagination alert to all sorts of possibilities beyond Goodland's offerings, beyond the nosiness of his real-life neighbours, especially beyond being stuck with Morris for a father for decades after his mother died too young.

Penny becomes a thousand women to him as well, thanks to reading about other women…so many women, sumptuous, tough, smart, crazy, each and every one sexy. He's never explained that to her, in so many words. He suspects it isn't entirely fair to her, to make love to the heroine of his current book in a way, in his head, but it also means he is never bored. Ever. He sighs happily and sinks into the dusty 19th century cattle drive on the page lit up before him.

The book-light wobbles. He shifts position from his

back to his left side and keeps one hand firmly pressed on the book which he places flat on the mattress. The light still wobbles.

He peeks around the curtain and can't make out a thing in the darkness. There is no moon and there are no lights on in Psycho's lean-to. There it is again. Wobbling and now a scratching.

The passenger door opens and the interior light comes on. A dark-haired woman with a heavily bruised face and one closed black eye jumps up into the seat.

"Hey!"

She crumples herself under the dash, barely closing the door but the light goes out.

Wade speaks calmly and quietly. "What are you doing in my truck?"

"I...I have...must get away from this place," the woman says.

"You might have knocked first," says Wade, whose adrenalin shakes are still subsiding.

"Wheel...," begins the woman but she keeps her head tucked down. Wade can hear her breathing rapidly, like a rabbit in a snare.

"Well," echoes Wade. He tries to think. "What are you running away from?"

"Dem men, bad peoples," she says, and looks up at him, her face a pale blur in the murky darkness but even so her black eye and split lip show up against her pale face.

"How long have you been here, in this place?"

"Oh...a couple day. Days," she corrects herself. "I gotta get away. You gotta help me get outta here. They gonna hurt me awful again if they find me!"

And then she tries to stop the hacking sobs that fill the cab.

He can't bear the ragged, raw sounds she is making. He eases himself out of the compartment and down into the driver's seat.

"Shhh, now. It's alright, we'll think of something, shhh," he says. "Why don't you get tucked away in behind there, where I was. You can pull that curtain shut, okay? I want to get the hell out of here myself but I've got to get the other driver back here first."

Her sobs halt slowly and she manages to raise herself from the floor and climb into the sleeping compartment. She is carrying one plastic grocery bag with hardly anything in it and she carefully removes her running shoes and puts them in the bag before swinging her legs up and into the nook. She groans a little as she stretches out and tries to pull at the curtain.

"I'll get that," says Wade.

"Tank you...very much. I am Manon St. Pierre," says the hoarse voice behind the curtain.

"Okay," says Wade. "Don't you worry, Manon. I'm Wade. I'll be back quick as I can."

He stuffs his feet into his boots and locks both doors.

Norman, if you balk at leaving for one second, I'm going without you. You want to hang out with these bikers, you can, but not me, fella. You can just forget it. I'll put your last pay cheque in the mail, bucko!

He picks his way down the trail in the inky dark toward the bonfire, hoping he'll be able to quickly spot the shape of Norman amongst all the others gathered around, swilling beer and balancing paper plates heaped with food. He stops well back from the light cast by the bonfire and several hanging lanterns and stares from group to group.

"Hey man!"

Wade jumps. He actually jumps to his left and bangs into a sapling tree.

"Norman! Scared the heck out of me! Just the man I needed to find. We gotta hit the road right now."

"Oh, no way man, I just ate and..."

"No," says Wade. "Can't discuss it here but I'm driving so you're either coming now or you're outta luck."

He turns, brushing by him, and heads back to the truck.

"Jeez, man, what's the big rush?"

"Talk later."

He can hear Norman thumping along behind him and he feels satisfied in a grim sort of way. He's finally stood up to him and calmly spelled out the way things are going to run around here. He should have done that a lot sooner on this trip.

"I'm driving," he says, unlocking the passenger door.

"Suit yourself," Norman says, sounding put out.

Wade starts the truck, giving the red and yellow knobs quick yanks to get the air pressure back up to snuff and then begins reversing simultaneously, counting on enough lingering pressure since their stop to keep the brakes operating. He stays in first gear with the headlights off, backing all the way down the narrow gravel road by the dull red glow of the tail-lights. He hears Norman start to say something and then stop himself. Good thing too.

He keeps on backing the rig for a hundred sweaty metres, seeing the faint glimmer of the bonfire to the right, between the sparse but massive Ponderosa pines, before he spots the wider grassy area he'd remembered when they drove in, a place big enough to swivel into and then get steering head first for the highway. He starts the turn, still using the big side mirror.

"Stop!" hisses Norman.

"Nope!" grunts Wade, hauling at the steering wheel, nearly done with the job.

"He's got a gun, for Chrissakes! Stop!"

And here are two of them, each armed and each coming to a window. Wade freezes, jamming a boot onto the foot brake. Norman rolls down his window.

"How goes it?" he hollers. "Be cool, man!"

The tall, skinny guy with scraggly blond hair and a beard and moustache to match waves his rifle in the air in a vague sort of way. Norman leans his arm along the window and looks down at the guard.

"Where you two goin' so late with that big truck?"

"We are late, man, seriously late for our next delivery. Just ask Psycho if you don't believe us. Love to stay and hang at the party, really would but work's work. Gotta hit the highway, man, or the clients will be mucho upset. We mean real upset, you know? Cool?"

The squat, dark man with a bandanna on his head says nothing, just scowls at Wade. He holds a cell phone in one hand, a rifle in the other. Which is worse? Wade begins to ponder this and then he hears a little mewing sound right behind him and his brain freezes again. He hopes his face looks glum and tired instead of freaked out and exhausted.

The blond man finally drops his scowl and lowers the rifle.

"Okay, I guess. Well…"

Wade puts his foot on the gas and lurches backward. *Shitshitshit!!!* He rams it into first and inches ahead, not looking at the men, concentrating on progressing as fast as possible through the eight speed gear box. Norman waves casually and the blond man yells.

"I'm not stopping," Wade mutters. "I'm not."

"What's your name?" yells the man, still trotting beside the truck.

"Gnaw-mun!"

"And Wade!"

Norman helpfully yells again, with another wave as the truck pulls ahead of the running rifleman. Wade takes a quick peek in the mirror and sees the blond man trip and fall, letting go of his rife and then trying to get back up onto his feet. He keeps his own foot jammed on the gas pedal and takes one more peek at the right hand mirror, seeing the dark-haired man yelling at his clumsy companion and pecking away at the cell phone in his paw.

Wade bounces them up onto the paved road in third gear and swerves, for what seems like a long, long, very long time into the oncoming lane before getting straightened out. He shifts down to second to gain some momentum again and his hands are slippery with sweat, sliding off the shift, grinding so damn loud a deaf hermit ten kilometres away can probably hear them. He hopes that the rock music is blasting every-one's eardrums out at the bikers' barbeque and that the surly guard's cell phone batteries have died simultane-ously with those of any phone at the receiving end.

He doesn't stop. He doesn't look both ways either.

He counts on seeing any headlights coming from either direction and he sees only darkness, so he takes the plunge and boots the truck and its heavy load away from fast bikes and long-range rifles and God only knows what else they have in their arsenal.

The intersection with Highway 3 comes into view with its big overhead lights. Normal cars and trucks zip by on the highway in both directions. The round sign of a gas station and restaurant glow. Normal. All is well. He breathes deeply at last and wipes his wet hands, one at a time, on his denim legs as he rumbles through Rock Creek, heading for the peaceful Kettle Valley.

*   *   *

1. Phone Kowalchuk and McCabe re: payment
2. Send receipts and thanks to Lafleur and Greene
3. Have Sean drive car here, then drop him off at home en route to post box
4. Put more Furazone on Mister Bojangles' wire cut
5. Make 6 pumpkin loaves and 6 dozen muffins for Saturday Market
6. Have two dozen or so good orange pumpkins ready for Market
7. Carve one of the pale long ones like Munch's Scream & make one round traditional grinner for display at Market
8. Do fabric inventory. If lots of autumn colours left, make a bunch of potholders and cinnamon

and clove hot-pads for Market-perfect for Thanksgiving dinners. Take extra hooks to hang stuff on.
9. Pack two boxes with raspberry jams and rhubarb as well as cranberry chutney for Market
10. Write Gwyneth and Gordon & send each a
new pair of potholders. Email Gordon recipe for
pumpkin muffins, per request
11. Go to Credit Union with local trucking
cheques & Wade's cheques, when they arrive
12. Find out how much a new phone with an answering machine and call display costs.

*   *   *

Aloysius Deacon drives in after calling to make sure she's
home and that his visit won't be a crucial interruption
of her work. He made it sound important, this need
to speak with her. Penny recalls the phrases "highly
confidential" and "not related to our history book at
all" which hung in the telephone air between them
and still lingers as she watches tall, spare Aloysius walk
up the driveway. He stoops, patting Casey en route,
talking to the dog whose demeanour switches from
suspicious watchdog to hulking lapdog with certain
visitors. Penny laughs at the sight of Casey's bowing
and grinning, his blue eye and brown eye crinkling
with delight as the old man sweet-talks to him.

"I happened to be sitting in Mark's Cafe yesterday,"
he says, putting down his tea cup with a sigh after
mowing through two of Penny's still warm chocolate

chip-dried cranberry cookies. "That new manager—looks about twelve years old—was being grilled by some supervisor from Prince George. This little toad was stressing the fact that none of the branches can give a loan of more than two thousand dollars to any customer, regardless of character and track record. It's all supposed to go by formula. They aren't trusted to know beans about people, just be able to follow the formula and send on any decisions of import to the head office. Well, we've all known that for ages but what happens next is these two financial Einsteins start discussing your ranch, the Toland estate, they called it, all the nuts and bolts, right there in a public restaurant! And I'm parked in the booth right behind them, minding my own business, having Mark's cherry pie à la mode and coffee."

Penny can hardly believe her ears. She stares hard at Aloysius, who is not crowing or smirking or anything smacking of a catty, gossipy attitude.

"What did they say and how many people could hear all this?"

"The supervisor had a loud yap and you could have heard a pin drop in there. Mark and his wife were working at the counter and about four other booths and tables had people. It was about 1:30, quarter to two, so most people had their lunches by then and a good thing too. He said the young manager had to keep an eye on that account, that Morris had run up a bunch of debt and taken out a mortgage for $125,000 only seven months before he passed and…oh Penny, I'm so sorry, that he put the ranch up against it and refused life insurance, claiming he had it elsewhere, and besides which, the property was worth close to half a million these days, even without a gas well on it."

Penny leans forward, her tea cup clattering madly in its saucer, fighting back a sour tea and chocolate wash of acid reflux at the back of her throat.

"It goes without saying, Penny, I will not utter one syllable of what I overheard but be prepared because who knows what interpretation all the other ears in Mark's Cafe will have made of this. If you want to make an official complaint, all the way to the top, I will sign your letter as a witness and we will get it notarized. I think you should switch all your dealings to another financial institution, if you don't mind me saying so, and that will help underline the importance of your letter and their appalling breach of privacy."

"Thank you, Aloysius, really, I mean, it's awful and it makes me so furious with both of them, and with Morris of course, as it was a complete shock to Wade and I. With the beef boycott last year, it could not have come at a worse time for us," she says. "I appreciate your discretion and the fact that you told me so quickly. I will take action, believe me."

She hardly knows where to start taking action first, in fact, and she needs to wait for Wade to get home and for the two of them to march in to the puppet manager's office to expedite the closing of their accounts after figuring out where to place them. Maybe write the angry letter first and see how they will respond. Don't throw the baby out with the bath water. We've banked there for decades. It's one stupid city manager breezing into a small town, having the upper hand, telling the young guy what's what, oblivious to the surroundings. We should have a serious talk with the young manager first, to see if he is at all aware of what confidentiality and privacy means in Big Butte.

*   *   *

Wade drives through the long night, taking anxious glances at his side mirrors, fearing a swarm of single headlights, knowing he will keep driving, no matter what. He will duck if they use rifles or handguns. He will drive over their black leather beer-gutted bodies and their chrome-laden bikes with a crunch and a squish if they try to ride in front of him. He will squash them like the spineless black sowbugs they are and he will take the rap for vehicular homicide and beat it in any sane courtroom in the country no matter how many mobbed-up lawyers they can afford to hire. His heart thwacks between his ribs like a running shoe in the dryer and he can't seem to get his breathing back to normal. Watching for bright animal eyes on the deserted highway going through more wide-open ranching country, he's making excellent time, really, the truck purring like a big lion through the black night.

They could pick him off easily as he crawled up some of these brutes of mountains in low gear, loaded like he is. He is grateful Anarchist Mountain is well behind them now, the mother of all climbs on the number 3 although the Salmo to Creston climb over the Kootenay Pass is nothing to sneeze at either.

Norman slumps in the passenger seat and snores mightily. Wade shoots him a cold glare. It was a matter of taking back control, he thinks, and it worked back there with Norman. It is his truck, after all and his goddamn business! Things were not going according to Hoyle on this trip and he has to look after himself and his truck and get them both home safe and sound.

Norman can take a permanent hike, in fact. He has thought long and hard enough about Norman and his future. Penny doesn't like the guy, not at all. Morris had been another story, of course; his father had jumped right into Norman's wise-cracking old soldier routine, like Morris had been one of the grunts alongside him in Vietnam as well. Morris welcomed Norman right off the bat and treated him like a real man, a guy who was entertaining; a regular man of the world.

It had been a relief, considering the only other option which was the old man being as scornful of Norman as he was of his own son on a daily basis. Wade remembers allowing himself a bit of credit for choosing to hire Norman on for the long hauls, before even seeing their buddy-buddy act in full swing. That should have been his first clue that something was amiss with Norman.

Sure, his father had co-signed the truck loan back in 1990 but it was a good deal at $25,000 Canadian, buying it down in Seattle. He'd paid it off in four and a half years, every cent and the five percent interest Morris had slapped on after the initial agreement.

Norman had made a few sputtering noises when he realized he couldn't use the sleeper, making it seem as though Manon had some nerve to hitch-hike with them and to sleep comfortably in the bargain.

"What the fuck, man," he'd started. "You got her outta there, fine, now there's no good reason she's gotta stay for the whole ride, izzit?"

Manon had begun to haul herself out, saying nothing, keeping her head down but he heard the small gasps she made as she struggled to move. He understood something then. He understood clearly that she was hurting in every cell of her body and he felt some old, familiar anger rise inside himself.

"Just drop me off where apples are. I mus' pick. I have only twenty dollar wit' me, is all," she'd managed to say.

"You never mind that," Wade had replied, loudly and firmly. "Get yourself some rest and I'll let you know when we get to Creston."

"Creston?" Norman had squawked.

"She needs to get a job picking apples. They've got late fall apples there, really good apples, and winter pears and such. It's on the way and she deserves a rest after what she's been through. Look at her face, man!"

Norman did not bother to look.

"Yeah, right!"

He'd sniffed, and shook his head, as if she'd been some wayward fifteen year old parading her brand-new booty down some small town main street instead of a tired twenty-two year old fruit-picker loaded down with a packsack, walking alone on an orchard side-road near Keremeos. When Wade asked if she wanted to press charges, if she wanted him to take her to the police station or at least go to the nearest hospital, she'd said no. Absolutely not.

So Wade keeps driving east, slowing down for

the deserted streets of the old coal-mining town of Greenwood with its handsomely painted and restored wooden buildings and the forlorn post-summer look of Christina Lake, climbing through the mountain passes, all alone in the dark except for a few other truckers and the odd car and he thinks, for the first time since leaving home four days ago, about Gwyneth.

His gut twists at the thought of his daughter being scooped up by a gang like that as she is walking home from teaching school some day. She is the type who would try to give them directions to the local Anglican Church if they asked. No. Why would he think she was that naive, that silly?

Gwyneth is like Penny, quick-thinking and sunny on the outside, hardworking and practical and a little too quick to worry about all kinds of stuff as well. She always works so hard at her lesson plans, making all sorts of extra things for her future elementary school classes during the summer. Graduation this coming spring.... She loves it and she'll be a great teacher.

She is so pretty, dark-haired and green-eyed like Mother's side of our family but with Penny's trim little build. Anyone can see that...and the way that some nutcases hang around campuses, knowing that some of the girls are from small towns, used to being friendly and helpful to all kinds of people.

Wade lets loose a held-in breath. He rolls his head around in a careful circle, clicking and crunching all the way, watching the two lane highway spool on ahead through the dense stands of tall trees on both sides. His jaw aches and he uses his left hand to push and pull at his lower face, easing some of the tightness there.

A murky bluish daylight hovers overhead when he eases the rig into the card-lock fuel station on the brightly-lit outskirts of Trail. Norman stirs, looks at his watch in a silent, surly gesture. Getting no response from Wade, he throws himself sideways in the seat and rams his head back on his rolled-up coat against the door.

Manon sticks her head out of the sleeper curtains as Wade swings back up into the driver's seat after fuelling.

"There is time for the bathroom maybe?"

"Yep. I was planning to stop at one of the fast food joints on the strip for something hot to drink. Can you hang on for a couple minutes?"

She nods and he notices how much her split upper lip is puffed up and how the blackened eye is now completely closed. He should have stopped sooner, back in Grand Forks maybe, if there had been some place open, and bought some ice. But she had been sound asleep then and he didn't stop, just shifted gears and purred his way down the pretty main street, shaded on both sides by giant, leafy trees, past the grand Victorian homes with their inviting verandas, underneath several blinking yellow traffic lights and then he was back on the highway again for another stretch. He ought to have insisted on the hospital, just plain insisted but she was so angry, so adamant about not going there. He will have a talk with her in Creston, a talk about diseases and how she must see a doctor there, and promise him that. Her poor face...and he can only imagine what he cannot see.

Just some chipped ice inside this cotton handkerchief will do, his mother would say, there's a good boy, thank you, sweetheart…

Wade sucks in a lungful of air and blows it out. Never on the face, she always put the ice pack on her chest or her ribs or stomach, though she tried to wait until he was out of the room, to hide it even more.

He drives down the lead, silver and zinc smelter city's fast food/vehicle lot/auto-body repair strip, looking for signs of life. He'll have to get hot chocolate, which he knows'll be sweet and insipid but he needs something hot and sweet to get him through the next stretch of driving. Unless he sees a place with really good coffee and then he'll get an extra-large. He'll buy something like that for her too and whatever she wants to eat, if she's able to eat at all. He is starving after missing supper last night, not that he's about to complain to anyone about that. He doesn't want to waste Penny's gingersnap cookies unless he has coffee to wash them down. He's already chewed on some rubbery cheddar cheese from the cooler, which is no longer cool. He needs ice for two reasons.

Norman stays put in the truck, resolutely in a pout or sleeping for real, he can't tell which. Wade is just happy to see an open sign ahead. Tim Horton's. Manon scoots to the washroom after asking him for a hot chocolate mixed with coffee. That sounds like a good plan so Wade buys two of those and a large double-double for Norman, fixed the way he likes it, in case he decides to wake up and be civilized about this situation. He buys the smallest container of Timbits and two breakfast muffins as well and then remembers to ask for ice.

"You'll have to go to the Mohawk station for that,"

says a young man with blue bags under his eyes at the till. "Sorry."

"I don't need a big bag though. Just a little, maybe a half-cup."

Manon comes around the corner just then with her face looking freshly washed and shiny-clean but with her black eye and mashed-looking mouth as well. A middle-aged woman behind the counter gives Wade a hard look.

He shakes his head and mouths. *Not me, not me!* He leans forward and touches his finger to his lips.

"I'm helping out a friend here and we need to move on pretty quickly. Just a half-cup of ice-cubes or chips would be a help to her right now."

The young man still has not noticed Manon waiting by the exit but the woman assesses Wade, makes up her mind and grabs a take-out cup. She goes back to the kitchen and returns with it, filled with chipped ice.

"Thank you, a whole lot," he says, adding it to the cardboard carrying tray. Manon carries the Timbits and they walk back in the ever-brightening dawn to the truck.

Norman has moved back into the sleeper while they were gone. Wade stares at the sound of genuine snoring behind the closed curtain. What a selfish absolute bastard!

Manon tugs at his jacket and shakes her head. She walks around the other side of the truck and grunts as she climbs up into the passenger seat. Wade fashions an ice pack out of one of his clean handkerchiefs and the ice chips and hands it to her. She smiles at him and winces at the same time before taking a sip of the mocha mix. Then she gently places the ice pack against her mouth and alternates sips of the hot drink with the cold treatment between her mashed mouth and her black eye.

Wade pops a sugar-glazed doughnut-round into his mouth before turning his attentions to the bacon and egg English muffin. Manon gingerly manages a chocolate Timbit.

"When did you last eat?"

"Oh, I don't know…quite a long time past," she says and turns away, but not before he sees the tears spill suddenly from her eyes.

"Are you sure you don't want to go to the police? Or a hospital? There's a big hospital here in Trail. I'll go in there to give you support if you want."

"No! What can they do now anyway? It's behind me, that. I just need to get far away from that place."

"How about I get you a milkshake then? A, let's see, it's called a frappe? It would be easier for you to eat and you're hungry, eh?"

She nods, and smiles carefully, moving the ice-hanky back to her lip.

"Thank you. A chocolate one, please."

He swings back down out of the truck and trots back to buy a large chocolate milkshake. The Tim Horton's woman beams at him as she hands it over and he smiles back. The tired young man avoids his eyes but Wade can feel him staring at him, maybe wondering what the real story is, maybe wondering why some men are so horribly mean to women and children, while some are so caring and kind and still others pretend nothing wrong is even happening.

Manon has difficulty with the straw at first but then she is able to hold it in the least damaged corner of her mouth. Norman is still snoring loud enough to wake the dead. No Timbits or sandwich or good hot coffee for the likes of him. Wade eases the truck out of the lot and follows the signs back to the highway heading east. He asks her to top up their mocha mixes with the large coffee he'd bought for Norman.

She is, she says, from Ile d'Orleans, near Quebec City, a beautiful place with historic houses, houses with special roofs that tourists came to see. Between her working command of English and Wade's rudimentary French, they cannot retrieve the right word for those roofs although her hands flash in squares and arcs attempting to recreate the shapes of the special roofs from home. She wanted, always, to see the Rocky Mountains and the Pacific Ocean and Tofino on Vancouver Island so she joined up with some chums after graduating to explore the west of Canada. Four years later, she is a veteran of the tree-planting and fruit picking crews in British Columbia and manages to spend a few months in Mexico every winter. But she'd fallen in love with a handsome man from Sherbrooke, who also liked to sleep with many other women she discovered, belatedly. He had grandly refused to use personal protection, promising her he would certainly look after a child, if one were to come along. Wade has an inkling she has just become pregnant with this freelance Romeo but he does not want to upset her by asking outright.

She'd walked away from him for good, late that Friday afternoon in Keremeos. She didn't notice the three bikers stopped at the side of the highway just before the farm road leading to the migrant worker shacks until they'd surrounded her. She will say nothing else except to reassure him that her wages went into the credit union there and she would be able to transfer them once she got to Creston. She shows him one of her running shoes and how she hides her social insurance card and her driver's licence as well as her bank card and a twenty dollar bill under the insole.

Three hours later the truck rumbles and hisses up and down the brutally steep Kootenay Pass. Wade keeps his eyes open for dangerous piles of fallen rock on the highway. He hopes to see mountain sheep, elk or moose but it is hunting season and the wild game has sensibly moved far away from the highway and the usual cavalcade of pick-ups packing two guys in bright orange get-ups and rifles on the ready for a lazy man's illegal window shot. It is cool and green and densely forested, this killer mountain pass, not that he has time for much sight-seeing. Manon is asleep. Norman does not stir. Road fatigue is settling deep into Wade's long and short bones, tired right through the marrow, as Grandma Amelia would put it.

Several dozen Canada Geese fly up from a grain stubble field on the left hand side of the highway over to the watery green sanctuary of the Creston Valley Wildlife Centre on their right. Rambling along a ridge above the valley floor, the sun is finally making head-way through a bank of solid charcoal clouds, glinting off tall grain elevators and the pretty orchard town of Creston.

The last image he has of Manon is from his side mirror: a jaunty wave and a lopsided smile as she stands beside the farm woman whose apple and pear orchards flank each side of the highway.

He'd stopped at her fruit stand because of her homemade sign on brown cardboard tacked to a hydro pole (PICKERS WANTED) and bought two cases of Jonagold apples, the fragrant red and gold-striped apples Penny loved second-best only to Gravensteins. As Manon slowly climbed down from the cab, he asked the woman if she was willing to take a chance on Manon. He leaned forward to whisper that he'd picked her up off the highway yesterday, on the run from some terrible treatment. He'd stressed that Manon needed to see a doctor to make sure everything was okay.

Mrs. Bidulka's face had briefly taken on a perplexed expression but then she launched into a rapid fire account of how her husband's number had just come up for his gall bladder operation, talk about lousy timing, but you couldn't turn it down else you'd wait another five months but he just had to have his bacon once a week and he'd suffer, by God, but he'd keep after the butter on his bread and cream in his coffee, too, wouldn't give it up, no sir, else life wasn't worth living and here she was desperate for reliable help herself. Yes, she'd said. Yes, she'd try the girl out, give her a break.

She'd given Manon's bruised face an alarmed once-over but then Wade was relieved to see a proprietary, compassionate expression take its place.

Manon had made her case convincingly. "I have pick apricot, cherry, apple, pear, grape, raspberry, strawberry, potato...and peach. The nectarine also."

"Goodness, young lady, with all that experience, you'll be well taken care of on our place. Guaranteed.

Let's get the paperwork done before more customers roll in. Can you get started this morning? You in any kind of shape to work then?"

And she'd turned to Wade and bobbed her head up and down fiercely as if daring him to say he had any doubts about her ability to defend Manon against all marauders. He told Manon to take care of herself. He could see tears filling up in her eyes again. He put his hand out for her to shake, knowing that a hug would hurt even if he was a huggy type of guy.

"We'll just get some arnica salve on that eye of yours first. Want some breakfast? Could scramble you up some nice, fluffy eggs in a jiffy. Mah-non, is it? Like some apple juice? Make tons of our own here. Drive a tractor? Yes? Good. Well, you could be a godsend, the week I'm having..."

Now, he looks back in the mirror at them, standing there waving as he heads for Cranbrook while Norman drives beside him, staring at the mountains ahead, silent as a glum, grey slab of rock.

No order for bulk apples here at the usual place either. Very odd. Norman says something about how they'd have had to keep them apart from the potatoes because the ethylene gas released by the apples made potatoes go rotten. But one compartment was packed full of potatoes, the other had the honey for Cranbrook and most of the remaining salmon packs, so there was lots of room left in that one for a big order of apples. No ethylene gas worries at all with two completely separate loads on the trailer behind them and only one twenty-four hour stretch ahead before they were home. Hardly enough time, never mind the distance between the loads, to make the spuds turn so fast. Wade keeps after him about it but Norman sticks to his story.

"No goddamn apples, I tell ya and if you don't believe it, phone the people yourself," he snaps at Wade. "Hey! They got a better source maybe. Who knows? I wasn't gonna rag on them to buy a little load from us as a favour which is all it is."

Wade feels his jaw clench again and he knows he needs to call his bluff or else stew about it for days or months.

"Yeah, you know what, Norman? I do need to call about it because if the North Peace Co-ops won't take them maybe the South Peace group will. Pull up at that little cafe we've gone to in Erickson, just up ahead here, so you can grab a bite to eat and I can make this call."

"Whatever. Fill your boots," he says, not even bothering to disguise his contempt.

*   *   *

7:05 a.m. call.

Can she possibly take on the high school home economics classes, both foods and clothing, for the rest of the week? There is a possibility of one more week depending on recuperation time for the teacher as well. A medical leave. The high school in town. A three-quarter hour drive, one-way.

It's the first time the high school has phoned her in the fifteen years she's been subbing in the district, always with the caveat that she couldn't guarantee being available for same day subbing on morning calls from town, like this very one.

Yes, yes! She can be there by quarter to nine. Thank you very much for calling!

She runs to the chicken house, sloshes the straw and manure-filled water out of the two halved car tires and refills them with clean water from the hose along with more feed wheat and oyster shell. She keeps running, turning Mister Bojangles out into the corral after dumping chopped oats and a slab of alfalfa hay into his manger. Taking just one moment to lean her head against his sweet-smelling shoulder and giving his neck a vigorous massage under his mane.

The barb-wire cut under his front fetlock is healing beautifully. She carefully spreads more Furazone on the wound. No trace of heat, therefore no nasty inflammation. He whickers at her when she leaves him in the corral.

"Mister B., you've got food, water, shelter and medicine taken care of. And a big, old barn and bigger corral all to yourself…Oh! I get it! You're just a lonely boy, lonely and blue, is it?"

She stops again to rub his lovely, slightly concave face, tracing the little whorl of hair in the centre of the perfect white diamond on his forehead.

"Dishy boyo, maybe I'll let you out with your harem tomorrow. Just heal that foot up first!"

She plants a kiss above his nose and turns to trot to the pig-pens for another burst of fresh water and food dispensing to the four weaner pigs all snuffling and whoofing a welcome. Then the final dash to the house, to shower for three minutes and jump into her navy blue gaucho skirt with a quilted bolero vest over a light blue shirt, navy tights and her navy blue leather flats.

On impulse she grabs her sewing basket and the bag of sorted fabric pieces for the Harvest Fair work she'd been planning to get to today. In the kitchen, after digging out a frozen bone for Casey from the deep freeze, dumping dry kibble into his big metal bowl and fresh water into his pail, she tosses a chunk of cheese, a wizened apple, several fresh carrots and a cheese and green onion scone into a couple of plastic containers. No time for coffee.

The Dodge coughs into life and wheezes for the first little while, gradually clearing its arteries enough to sway and float, in its disconcerting fashion, down the road to town. She will ask Sean if he knows anything about the spongy steering or suspension or whatever it is once she survives this week. Meanwhile, she is grateful to him for fixing the starter because she could never have taken on this assignment otherwise.

She taps the brakes a few times as she coasts down the hill past the Community Hall and Fairgrounds, past the log church, pausing at the 4-way stop, and then swaying past the Legion and the Co-op Store. The speed limit is 50 km on this deserted stretch. So far, she's only met one mud-covered half-ton carrying welding gear. The clock is defunct on the car dashboard but when she looks at the series of displays more closely, her heart sinks. The gas needle is on empty.

How can that be? Surely Sean didn't go roaring around the country with it? No, Hazel wouldn't allow that and nor would Stan. What on earth happened to the full tank of farm gas she'd filled it up with last week before she found out it wouldn't start?

The odometer doesn't work either so that is no use checking. She groans out loud and pulls a U-ee to head back to the pumps at the Co-op. She has to wait behind two grain trucks which have come out of nowhere to fill up while two gas field vehicles nudge in behind her. Hovering, nearly on her knees, she inspects the gravel under the gas tank, sniffing for a leak and staring at nothing out of the ordinary there. She lurches back up, her school clothes still immaculate.

This is taking forever. The Willard's grain truck must have been running on vapours judging by the time it's taking to fill up. Then she notices the lights going on in Evie's coffee kiosk and the shutters swinging open. She marches over, grateful for this little gift, greets the rumpled morning face of Evie Granger and asks for a large regular coffee to go, two per cent milk, even though she would have loved to splurge on the biggest latte, a double shot, but she's not about to part with the best part of five dollars. Penny drinks the excellent regular coffee and waits for her turn at the pumps with more poise and equanimity.

When she finally sticks the nozzle in, the damn thing pings full after $5.21. Hell's bells! Now her gas gauge doesn't work anymore either! She moves the car out of the way and runs into the Co-op to dump loonies and assorted other coins onto the counter while Myra Duncan yaps on to Louisa Granger about one of her kids who wants to quit school and get a job in the oil-patch. She blats on in a motherly tone of mingled aggravation and pride about her sixteen year old baby boy.

Penny wants to smack a yardstick across that enormous protruding gluteus maximus encased in skin-tight denim. Your Jordan is so dyslexic he can hardly read or write or think and you and your ignorant husband refused to understand or accept it, much less help him out for all these years since he was tested in Grade Two! Now he's another male Duncan oaf all primed to get himself killed while driving drunk before the age of eighteen right after he impregnates a couple of fourteen year olds. Shut the heck up and move before I lose it!

"Here's the right change, Louisa, I'm late, sorry!" she butts in, not sorry at all but fed up.

Penny is fed up with mechanical things that don't work, with yappy, slow people, with grain trucks going 42 kilometres an hour down a 55 mph straight stretch with another grain truck crawling out of a field into the oncoming lane just as she is attempting to floor the gutless Dodge Dart past the sluggish lummox in front of her.

She jumps on the brakes more than half a dozen times as she lurches over the newly paved river road and up the Poplar Canyon shortcut into town. She is sweating and nervous and pissed off all at once.

She takes deep breaths, looks at her watch as she crawls past the RCMP station on the outskirts of town.

"You're okay. Fourteen minutes to go. Home-room and then a spare. Relax. It's perfect. You'll get your bearings."

She talks herself into calmness and deftly wheels the car into the staff parking lot. Using the car mirror, she blots her face with one of Wade's spotted blue cotton handkerchiefs, slashes the nub of some waxy pink six year old lipstick across her lips, smacks them together and heaves herself out of the car, both hands loaded down with bags.

Bypassing a student line-up at the office counter, she pops around the corner and invades the secretarial sanctum. Ten minutes to spare.

"Hi, I'm Penny Toland, subbing for Anna Schmidt this week. Can you please direct me to her home-room and whoever has her lesson plans for me and so on?"

The young woman with short, blonde curls looks over at the other woman, an older redhead with a shellacked coif the likes of which Penny hasn't seen since 1968. She is in the thick of dealing with the line-up of students. The blonde sighs, putting down a stack of slips.

"Ms. MacLeod knows all about that, I think…"

"I've driven in from Goodland because I was called just this morning. I'm later than I'd like to be and I'd like to get organized as soon as possible."

Penny starts out tentatively but finishes with a definite flourish. What is it with people who stonewall for no apparent reason but to avoid doing anything to solve a minor problem? Maybe the senior secretary, now giving a sullen teen hell for not bringing in a note to explain his spotty attendance record, is a dragonish control freak. But that is beside the point.

She has classes to teach, new equipment to get familiar with. She might even need to do a major shopping expedition so that the foods classes can function normally today and God knows what else. Penny lets out an exasperated sigh and stares at the young woman who is now avoiding her gaze and nervously clicking her manicured nails together, done in that squared French style which is all wrong for her small, plump hands. She glances up from her computer and smiles quickly, revealing tiny, pearly teeth and a set of dimples.

"But let me see where Mr. Riordan is, the Vice. He'd have Anna's stuff. Her home-room is in the new wing, Room 201, to the left and straight down to the end of that hall, then left again. I'm Candy. My boyfriend farms in Goodland. Tom Good? You know him? His parents are Joe and Maggie? Here, I'll get you to the Staff Room."

Penny trots after Candy, who chatters about Tom the whole while, as she escorts her to the staff room which is connected to the front office by a corridor leading past a long row of staff mailboxes and the offices of two vice-principals, two counsellors and the principal. She can hear a girl crying in one office and a woman raising her voice in the principal's lair. Tough years, the teens. Penny takes another deep breath.

"Here you are, Ms. Toland," Candy announces. "Hope you have a good week. I'm coming out to the Harvest Dance at Goodland Hall this weekend. See you there?"

"Oh, no, I don't think my husband will be back by then or if he is, he'd likely be too tired. But you never know."

As she opens the staffroom door, a gaunt, be-spectacled man with a salt and pepper brush-cut and a perturbed look on his face steams through.

"Oh, Mr. Riordan, this is Ms. Toland, subbing for Ms. Schmidt?"

He stops, motioning her to follow him inside. His

face relaxes and he smiles broadly. Penny deposits her fabric bag onto an armchair just in time to meet his outstretched right hand for a brisk hand-pumping session.

"Just the person I need to meet. Thank you for coming in on such short notice. It's a bit of a drive, I know. Anna had to go in for emergency surgery very late last night, appendicitis, and we're having a hard time getting subs for some of our classes. Very glad you can handle home-ec for us here. Now, let me get her notes, she's very meticulous, I think you'll be fine…"

He wheels around and waves one long arm at the fridge and coffee area and swings it around to encompass the coat racks and bathrooms as well as the sofas and chairs spread throughout the large windowless room.

"Make yourself at home here. You know the drill, I'm sure."

Penny quickly puts her lunch in the fridge and steps around a silver-haired, pony-tailed man making coffee. Riordan is still talking about her home-room and how some of the students in her group have permission to leave immediately after attendance is taken to catch a bus for the Honours 10 Science oil refinery field trip this morning. Then he repeats the information about Anna Schmidt's recuperation time and how he hopes that if things work out for her she can commit to subbing the rest of this week and possibly next week as well. And would she please stop by his office before the end of the day to let him know her plans.

She looks up and meets the gaze of the coffee-making teacher, who has turned around, cup in hand. He raises a dark eyebrow and gives her a head-tilting, quizzical look and a nice smile. She allows a quick nod and smile in response. Lordy, gorgeous blue eyes!

Heading over to the door where Riordan is waiting, she takes the big red coil binder containing Anna Schmidt's lesson plans and attendance records and a set of keys from him.

"Thanks," she says brightly and gives him a smile that she hopes is reassuring and competent. "Room 201, down the hall, right?"

"You got it!" he booms, looking completely relieved now. One more administrative problem solved. He gives her a cheery half-salute as she turns and speeds toward her classroom, dodging clumps of students while the first notes of an electronic bell echo musically in the corridors.

Later, driving home, she turns on the tape deck, one of Gordon's legacies to the Dodge Dart, and harmonizes happily all the way home with the late, great Hoyt Axton. Boney Fingers and Sweet Misery and the rest of his golden oldies. She pats the stack of potholders beside her that she'd made during the lunch hour in her sewing classroom, using a magnificent new Pfaff with all the bells and whistles.

The students had been very good, except for one Grade Ten group of girls who were classic little bullies but all she did with them was lean over their table and whisper 'I'll do the demonstration now with your help'. They'd looked around frantically at each other then, black-rimmed eyes agog.

("Oh, no, it's like she's gonna be standing here and doing her lesson stuff, like, right here with us for this whole, entire class! That so, like, sucks!")

She smiles, remembering how they'd quickly adapted to being almost the centre of attention as they handed her spatulas and found the right cake pans and preheated the oven. Celebrity chefs in the making. The sampling session of the demo carrot cake afterward was a big hit too, apparently something Ms. Schmidt didn't indulge them with.

"Yeah, she takes all our food to the staff room and the teachers all get to pig out on it, that's what happens!"

The cluster of variously streaked and dyed hairdos had all bobbed up and down.

"So unjust. Like, it's our food."

"Rilly."

"We made it, eh?"

And after class, in the hallways, several of them had beamed at her shyly and murmured, 'Hi, Ms. Toland' as they flounced by in their little packs and posses.

Penny basically likes teenagers, at least ninety-nine percent of them. She will definitely be back, working here more often if the rest of the week progresses like today's classes. She had stipulated to the School Board office years ago that she couldn't do any early morning calls for just one day's work in town during the winter months. That had resulted in no calls at all from the town schools in the past fifteen years. Nobody knew her so no one could spread the word about her competence and rapport with the kids and so she was limited to the Goodland elementary school, hoping and praying for three days of work there a month. Today's experience has, at long last, demystified the urban experience and she intends to let the Board office know that she will be available from now on. She wants to be on the list and if there is a blizzard, she will turn an assignment down but at least her name will occur to people like the vice-principal. One week, maybe even two! Oh, this is perfect, thank you, thank you!

She just can't be away from home, away from the animals, for longer than twelve hours. She absolutely cannot be stuck in this town, looking for a cheap motel, with the road home closed by a blizzard, which happens at least two or three times every winter.

She pulls into the yard at 4:45 p.m., has the chores done by 5:30 p.m., makes an omelette for supper and after brushing her teeth, she jumps back into the car and drives to St. Matilda's for the first choir practice of the new season.

She'd nearly convinced herself that she could miss it this once, what with chores and working in town and the long day she'd already put in. Then she'd reminded herself how singing for two hours felt, how the worries of her world receded as she focused on breathing and pitch and following the sheet music. It was hard on her tired feet but good for her soul.

Sure enough, just the sight of the familiar cars and pick-ups parked outside the log church lifts her spirits. She can hear the laughter and hub-bub of twenty-six singers who'd all driven many kilometres to be here. The mix of vocal tones reminds her of the welcome she receives in the hen-house every morning, the cooing and cawing exclamations, the chicken vernacular for hi's and how are ya's and it's about time, we're starving in here! Followed by the puck-puck-pucking of a contented flock at the sight of their purveyor of food and water and light and fresh air. An egg-robber, true, but an utterly reliable one who provides all the requisite creature comforts.

Penny steps into her usual soprano spot between Carol Jackson and Donna-Jean Granger. Judith Maisonneuve has plugged in their new state of the art portable keyboard, the reward for eight months of determined fund-raising, and flexes her fingers over the keys. St. Matilda's ancient pump-organ wheezes like an asthmatic and simply cannot manage the faster, more complex pieces. For almost a decade Judith had been able to work her magic with a very basic electric keyboard from Carey Lafleur's teenage son, who'd abandoned his early rock star ambitions. They'd soaked off the neon decals of skulls and vampires and heavy metal band logos first.

Judith had made do with it until she could no longer tolerate keys suddenly going mute in mid-concert. Because she was much in demand, playing for a highly regarded Big Butte chamber ensemble and for her own church congregation, St. Cecilia's Catholic Church in town, Francine Young warned her confidants in the choir that they had to somehow find Judith a proper instrument. 'Or', she'd grimly told Penny on the phone one day, 'We will lose Judith and this whole choir might go down the tubes.'

So the choir members had launched themselves at the regional arts council for grant-in-aid status, they charged more when they sang for weddings (but still sang for free at funerals), and they sponsored many raffles (a logging truck load of firewood, a side of beef, dinner for four at the Aurora Restaurant, a weekend for two at the new luxury Spruce Chalet Inn, a $100 gift certificate from Top to Toe Aesthetics and a mint green and pale yellow confection of a baby quilt, the latter contributed by Penny). They exceeded all fund-raising expectations and Francine socked away the excess for future road trips to choral festivals, more sheet music, workshop instructors and the annual donations to the church for the use of the building.

Penny feels a little thrill as the notes cascade in a tricky decrescendo. Donna-Jean winks at her as Judith moves into an even flashier bit of business, switching to a pipe organ program to transport them all to a massive cathedral, getting them revved up for singing for the first time together since the May spring concert. Penny had not requested them for Morris' funeral, which was a small and private family affair, attended by exactly nine people.

Carol nudges her with an elbow and directs her attention to Gloree Olsen who is swaying her ample hips to the music, eyes closed, blissful smile on her lips. Penny stifles a little giggle, coughing into her hand and looking away. Gloree enjoys a nip or three of white wine of an evening. As long as she doesn't show up pickled on concert evenings, Francine will tolerate her. Likewise, burly Dane Eisler, their best bass-baritone, binges regularly on booze but he hauls himself down to Monday evening choir practices and to all the concerts absolutely sober, if haggard, after his weekend blow-outs.

Penny scans the rest of the familiar faces, nodding and smiling at those who catch her eye. No new members this season. Francine had advertised for more bass and baritone voices as well as tenors in the *Goodland Gazetteer*, their bi-monthly community newsletter online and off, but so far, no results, it seems.

Francine makes her way to the raised dais and flaps her arms at the motley collection of individuals gathered to offer their voices for the Goodland Community Choir. She is a brave woman, thinks Penny, and not for the first time, as the happy gabble ceases and the singers pay attention.

Five men, twenty-one women. Three bass-baritones and six tenors, including three women. Nine altos and eight sopranos, including three who are actually altos but are not able or willing to switch from singing melody all their lives to singing in the alto section. Average age fifty-two years old. About a dozen of them can read music and the rest have good ears or have finally learned not to bellow like repressed opera soloists.

Their black and gold music binders are passed from pew to pew and Francine reels off the dates for their winter concerts and tells them about an invitation to a choral festival in Prince George early in the new year. She's chosen another challenging array for them, always pushing them well past their comfort zones, far beyond the cherished old chestnuts. Christmas hymns in French, Spanish, Latin and German as well as English. Thankfully, thinks Penny, they are repeating the ever-popular "Hallelujah Chorus" and the gorgeous "Magnum Mysterium" which they'd performed four or five years earlier.

"Let's do a good warm-up tonight, people!"

Francine nods at Judith who swiftly provides the regular piano program and off they go, up and down the octaves, singing the scales, swelling and subsiding, clearing their dusty, rusty throats, breathing deeply and letting their voices flow and blend with each other.

A wind from the north bears down on the thick spruce grove, planted by chilled parishioners in the 1930's, which surrounds the log church. The wind swirls around them and over them. Penny can see bright bronze and gold poplar leaves twisting in little spirals outside the arched church windows, several lightly skittering against the leaded glass as the last of the autumn daylight fades to black.

In the breaks between their singing, she can hear the wind's repeated attempts to push through the windbreak, puffing around the belfry high above, testing the wood shingles on the roof. Tears suddenly fill her eyes and, skipping a few notes, she ducks her head down, brushes them away and takes another deep breath.

Release, that's all it is! Just letting go of a few worries with a few healthy tears. Clearing out toxins and tensions. She knows that. But don't be maudlin, girl. Get a grip. Tomorrow afternoon I'm supposed to meet with the Historical Society but I can't. Must tell Georgie or Bert here tonight, to let the rest know, and that I'll call Edna tomorrow in the early evening to catch up.

*   *   *

Norman roars and wakes Wade up.

"Gotta do the scales, man!" he bellows over his shoulder at the sleeper where Wade has just spent two solid, satisfying hours. Why wake me up for something so routine, he wants to holler back? Stop your damn yelling!

"'S' okay, take 'er in," he mumbles. No problems. They are less than 10,000 kg and the load is evenly distributed. He sinks back, desperate for more sleep.

The swaying wakes him next. It isn't pleasant, sustained movement like the endlessly comforting rolling and clacking of a railroad car across the prairies, like the dream he'd been having about a rare, early family trip away from the ranch they'd taken with the kids, across Canada by train from Edmonton to Montreal. This is a sickening kind of lurching and braking that his body responds to, dragging his mind out of the dream. This time he yells out loud.

"Norman? What's going on?"

"Bad winds, man! I'm just thinking about pulling over. Some of the other guys have pulled over already. Got us some woolly, weird-ass winds here. Don't like it."

He starts downshifting, his thick paws busy with the air-brake knobs.

"Okay, wait it out," Wade yawns and closes his eyes again. He rolls over and hears something crackle beneath him as Norman eases the truck to a standstill. He rolls back and searches through the pockets of the coat he'd thrown on top of himself just after Creston.

The edge of an envelope pokes out of the inside pocket. Sonuvabitch! The island cheque! Not to mention the biker's payment! Cranbrook's done, he'd stayed awake for the transaction there but they always made a direct deposit to Northern Gold Honey Farms, the apiary back home that would pay Wade for all his work on their behalf, also by direct deposit, no cheque, so it hadn't crossed his sleep-stunned brain. It was a relief to make an efficient stop with the usual Co-op gang to deliver honey only, then to welcome the dazzling sun spreading over the wide Columbia valley with the white-capped mountains marching alongside, flanked by deep green swaths of conifers and gold aspens fluttering their last farewell of the season. This is another place they could have lived, in another life, maybe…

They are running late again though, due to Wade's call to the northern co-ops and subsequent two hour detour to pick up one thousand kilos of Braeburn and Gala apples in Creston. Wade doesn't share with Norman what the manager tells him about not being contacted at all. How she'd tried to leave a message for Wade but couldn't because the message machine wouldn't pick up and how frustrating it was not to get hold of him. She'd never heard from Norman at all. But she was still keen to buy apples and the Creston grower was also mightily relieved, Wade could tell, even though there was no cheque for him to hand over, as usual. The Co-op manager was making arrangements to quickly send payment to him. All was now well, except for the Norman M.I.A. part.

They must be somewhere in the Rogers Pass now, for winds like this. They have somebody to talk to in Revelstoke apparently and then the final drop-off for honey and some salmon in Kamloops. Lordy, at this rate he'd beat the envelope home. In fact,…but his sleep-soaked brain retrieves the memory of the pursed lips and sharp eyes of Penny giving him instructions to mail them to her no matter what.

If he could hang his head, if he wasn't already flat on his back, he would. This is why she gets so angry with him and why she'll be steaming like a forgotten tea-kettle, sighing, fuming, and silently homicidal. He'd meant to send the damn things, half a dozen times they'd crossed his mind, but this trip is so out of the ordinary that the notion of stopping in some peaceful, orderly little town, seeing the flag flying over the tidy red brick post office and following through, well, it just wasn't that kind of trip. He closes his eyes and feels the rig rocking and hears the cross-winds howling, spattering dust and chips of gravel all over them.

Norman has Maria Callas cranked up on the tape deck. The Verdi arias. Wade hums with his eyes closed. He needs more sleep. When he opens his eyes again, the world wobbles. He tries to raise himself up and flops back. Tries to talk. Can't. Woozy brain. Thick, tired tongue.

What's this?

Heavy pelting racket on the metal roof.

"Jeez Murphy, man! Hail as big as banty eggs goin' on out there!"

Wade heaves himself up to look out the curtains. Sure enough, the entire highway is white with bouncing pellets of hail. One smacks the windshield with an alarming thunk.

"Double-yolker," shrieks Norman.

Wade scans the windshield looking for new cracks or starter stars. There are two major cracks already, courtesy of northern pea gravel the size of baseballs and at least six little stars. One new one, so far as he can tell, not too big. He has to get this attended to as soon as he gets back. He doubts an inspection would pass him like this. There! He spots another new irregular star, too big, spreading on the windshield. More ice chunks hammer down. He hangs his head now, stifling a groan.

A small red Firefly with Alberta plates drives up the hill toward them and skids to a stop only metres away, right across from the truck. Two large young men stare up at them, laughing. There are duffel bags and boxes and sleeping bags stuffed behind the young giants in their tiny car.

"Now that's effin' intelligent!"

"I'll get out and tell them to move," says Wade.

"Nah, I'll give 'em a taste of the horn and maybe they'll figure it out," growls Norman and commences blaring the horn and making emphatic hand gestures signifying 'move the hell forwards or backwards because you've just created a single lane on top of a blind rise, you stupid morons!'

They look blankly at him, shrugging their shoulders and making faces that convey puzzlement and more than a hint of scorn. Norman opens the door and Wade reaches over and puts his hand on his shoulder. Norman shrugs it off.

"I'll just go over there and wipe those stupid looks off their faces and toss that tin can of theirs in the ditch while I'm at it!"

"Get a grip on yourself, man! You could get arrested!"

"Yeah? By what? The Mounties are gonna come riding over the ridge?"

"Hold on, Norman. They're kids, they're trying to be cool now but they've probably pissed their pants trying to drive in this. Look, they're driving away. Save your powder, man!"

"For what?"

Not waiting for an answer, Norman slams the door shut. Callas soars and a heavy gust of wind rocks the truck. The hail stops as suddenly as it started.

You weren't such a big defender for a beaten-up, gang-raped woman, you asshole. Mr. Buddy-buddy with those scuzzy bikers. No, you're going to try being a big man for someone who really needs some muscle. Pound out a couple of eighteen year old kids heading for B.C.

"Just drive on as best you can, take 'er easy, okay, Norman?" says Wade. "Wake me up in Revelstoke. At the scales if they're open. Or the card-lock if we need fuel. Whichever comes first. Thanks."

He yanks back the curtains and sinks back onto the foam mattress. He exhales mightily. He can smell himself, the sour stink of his own stale sweat. The music is too loud to ignore, impossible for his exhausted brain to override. So he lies there for a long time with his eyes open, his guts in a knot, trying to get his breathing to settle down. When it does, when he lets the sourness inside and outside go, only then can he close his eyes.

The young girls, about six of them, surrounded him and held on to each other's hands, beginning a slow spin around him. They were all smirking, staring at him, undulating their unripe bodies, spinning faster. He tried to laugh, it was a game, right? They were only ten or eleven years old, goofing around with the strange man. They shouldn't be doing this. Where are their parents? Inside the hall. Dancing. Getting stoned.

He said, 'Ha.' Flat-sounding, unfunny. Then, 'excuse me please' and he plunged between two small arms, feeling too big, too mean to play Red Rover but they wouldn't let him out and he had to get away. They squealed and yanked their hands apart, shrieking obscenities at him. He ran behind the hall and turned on the tap of the big rain barrel. How did he know it was there? Good water. He stuck his head under the tap and drank and let the gush of it pour over his face, using his hands to scoop more behind his neck, then drinking some more. Finally, he felt better, cleaner, cooler. He thought he could sleep well now.

*   *   *

URGENTLY NEEDED:
Indigenous clay for on-site digging. Preferably less than one-half hour's drive from school. Contact: Frederic Murdoch, Art Dept.
THANK YOU!

She pauses in front of the bulletin board, sipping her tea and waiting for the principal's afternoon announcements on the P.A. system to end. She turns her ears off to his recitation about which National Hockey League teams were playing that evening.

"Attention All Teenagers: Are You Invincible, Immortal & Infertile?!"

Yes, that announcement would get their attention. Still, it's been a good week for her although she hasn't heard about Anna's expected return date from at-home convalescing which is why she's still waiting around to meet with Riordan. She'd like to have headed home at the start of her fifth class, a lucky spare, but instead she sewed eight more quilted hot-pads to fill later with shreds of cinnamon bark and pounded whole cloves and allspice. She'll be able to present a nice little display at the Farmers Market booth tomorrow after all, thanks to squeezing in sewing during lunches and spares.

"So I hear you run a ranch with a river running through it, to paraphrase a movie based on a book title," purrs the voice in her ear.

She forces herself to turn around slowly although her tea has already slopped onto her startled hand.

Mister Blue Eyes. Somehow she knew he'd be the art teacher. Could have been the casual flaunting of the unwritten staff dress code. No shirt and tie. Paint blotches on his black high-top runners (dead giveaway) and completely relaxed all-black clothing (ditto). Not to mention the silver ponytail and great tan.

"Frederic Murdoch," he says and makes a little bow. *Free-deric*.

"Penny Toland," she says, clutching her mug of tea. What do you want from me, she wonders?

"Would you happen to know if, on that land of yours, there are any sizeable clay deposits? Especially, say, deposits in the river banks that an all-wheel drive vehicle could drive fairly close to?"

"Hmm. We've got lots of sand and gravel but I'm not sure...I haven't ever looked for it, myself. The top-soil is mainly sandy loam..." She trails off, thinking, mentally scanning the long line of cutbanks along the Muddy. Where, now, where? Yes.

"You might try driving to where the old bridge used to be. You can still see the remains of it very well, she says. "Anyway, I think there are very solid yellow banks there, on the north side. It's only fifteen minutes from town if you take the airport road and then turn north at the T-junction."

"Is that old road still open though?"

"Well, you have to take your chances."

Penny sets her tea mug on the counter and points at the large scale map of the school district on the wall.

"It's been officially closed for nearly a year and those banks are riddled with springs so they're constantly slumping and sliding."

She traces the route, following the thin, broken grey lines of the old road to the Muddy River's blue meandering line.

"This is definitely 4x4 terrain or impassable where it's washed out so look it over well first so you don't get into a bad spot. Were you planning to take your classes?"

"Yes, but I'd want to scout the sites first, see if the kids could spread out and dig properly along a wide seam."

The staff room door slaps open and a red-faced Riordan comes steaming into the room, clutching a couple of file folders. He ignores them both and falls into one of the armchairs to quickly riffle through the papers.

Frederic raises his eyebrows again and returns his gaze to her. Penny takes a half-step backward and bumps against the metal lip of the bulletin board.

"You've been very helpful. Though I was hoping to pay a visit to a real ranch," he says.

What an outrageous flirt! Doesn't the ring here on my left hand give him a clue at all?

She decides to play this one very straight. Then she decides not to be an uptight country hick. Then she thinks she is probably seeing and hearing things that weren't even intended. Projection, the kind of thing teenagers and control freaks do to contort the true intentions of others.

"If I knew of any accessible clay on our place," she says, picking up her tea mug again, "it would be fine with us if your art classes came out to dig it up. Provided it isn't in a tricky spot, of course. Wade and I live a good three-quarters of an hour drive from here though," she says. There, I whacked the ball into no-man's-land for you, Romeo.

If anything, he turns up the wattage in the smile. He has very white teeth and very tanned, still youthful skin. That dramatic silver hair of his is premature but it suits him, she can't help noticing. The contrast is so striking. Her own sandy brown mop has offered up a few mundane iron-grey strands lately.

"Well, if the stuff down by the old bridge is too difficult to get to with a vehicle, I may need to look further afield," he says. "I'm new here, just started in September and I've had no other leads this week what-soever, so thank you."

And then he turns and scoops up several bags and a large portfolio case.

"Have a good weekend," she calls out. Keep this nice and light.

"Thank you. You too."

Another big smile and wave. He tosses a well-worn black leather jacket over one arm and lopes out the door. She can't help noticing the solid set of shoulders and compact little derriere nicely filling out the black denim jeans.

Riordan glares after him and then fixes his beady brown eyes on her.

"Thank you for working this week, Penny. If you can manage three more days next week, Anna should be back on her feet for next Thursday she says. Does that suit your schedule?"

"I can manage that," she says, her heart lifting. Thank you, thank you! Got the mortgage and machinery payments all covered for October and November!

"Anna tells me she usually gets the next week's shopping done during this Friday spare, this one just now, of course," Riordan says, looking miffed. "So you're on your own, I'm afraid, planning-wise for those three days at least. She's got accounts set up at all three of the big grocery stores in town and at Suzanne's Fabrics for the clothing classes so just do what you need to do there. I'm really sorry about the late notice. She was sleeping this afternoon and well,...she's still recovering."

"It's okay, I understand," says Penny, her heart sinking.

"Thank you. Much appreciated," he says, nodding, still looking preoccupied and unhappy. He opens one of the folders.

A horde of teachers fills the room and Riordan jumps to his feet again, heading for the door, gripping the folders tightly to his narrow chest. Penny finishes her lukewarm tea with a little grimace and contemplates her options, listening to the happy Friday babble of the other teachers, yakking about meeting up with each other at the Legion or weekend pick-up basketball plans. Several women, including Rhoda Persky who'd given Penny a welcoming hug earlier in the day, were planning a baby shower for a colleague on maternity leave, a Saturday afternoon ambush in collusion with her husband. A very tired-looking young man uses the phone to promise someone he'll buy more diapers on the way home and pick something up for dinner too.

Penny grabs a quick refill of tea and heads back to the home economics lab. She throws open the cupboard doors, checks out the deep freeze and the oversized fridge, pores over the curriculum guidelines for the first half of the year and starts making a list.

Keep it simple, keep it fun, do something seasonal. Pumpkins! Yes, make curried pumpkin soup, served in its own shell. Make pumpkin muffins, pumpkin loaves, pumpkin pie and cheesecake if we can afford it. Do some carving along the way. Bring them in from home because the Goodland Co-op doesn't want or need them anymore and you've got way too many pumpkins on hand at home. Make a harvest wreath project in the sewing room and do the spice hot-pads if there's enough money to buy the spices in bulk for the Grade Tens. Anna's stocked up on lots of wreath-making material in there and I can improvise with more of my dried stuff from home as well, just to get through three days. She's written 'Drama Project-Edie in-class' for Monday, Grade 11 & 12. Don't have a clue what that's about but it sounds organized. She'll try to find Edie now or call her on the weekend so she knows for sure what to prepare for.

She would have appreciated this information much sooner and then she'd have made much better use of her spare instead of sewing up sixty-four whopping dollars worth of hot-pads. Now she'll have to do the shopping on a Friday afternoon along with everybody else in town. She'll be lucky to get home by seven o'clock. The weaner pigs will be shrieking their little heads off, so used to being fed at five o'clock on the dot every afternoon.

Still, hadn't she hoped for this? A good stretch of subbing will carry them well into the winter. She won't allow herself to sag about it. She'll treat herself to some take-out Chinese from Mark's Cafe on the way home.

No, she can't do that. Not yet. Wade still hasn't phoned and there hasn't been any cheque in the mail from him either. Maybe today, though.

Don't start! she thinks. Don't get all bent out of shape about it. He's only been gone five full days, no, six, counting the Sunday he left. Five mail days. More than enough time for at least one of them, the one from the coast, to arrive. And they were special delivery envelopes too! No. Don't start. It's going to be okay. But don't splurge today. Wait for some kind of pay cheque. Have it in your hands. Make a list first. Then celebrate a little. Think of Christmas. Think of Gordon and Gwyneth and surprising them with a tidy couple of cheques for the second semester. Think of emergencies for which we have no savings, like Mister Bojangles having a real problem, much more expensive than getting his foot caught while trying to paw through a barb-wire fence to reach a fresh clump of alfalfa!

There's a leftover roast chicken and boiled potatoes in the fridge at home.

*   *   *

The heavy snowfall begins in Albert Canyon, snow falling so thick and fast that both of them lean forward into the hypnotic screen. For a while, Norman tries high beams alternating with low beams to change the effect of the flurries temporarily and to ease their eye-strain. The heater in the truck reeks of old dust and diesel fuel exhaust. They debate whether to turn it off and freeze or turn it up full blast and crank down the windows to only partially freeze but with fresh air circulating at nose level. They opt for the latter strategy. At least their feet will be warm and they have no choice but to stay awake.

Norman steers the truck into downtown Revelstoke just as darkness is closing in on them, rumbling past the guardian grizzly sculpture on the main street, driving slowly. The highway has been gruelling, with the fleet of orange dump trucks just starting to lumber along, spreading sand and salt on the Trans-Canada. The Rogers Pass was a snaky black ribbon of icy ball bearings. Norman pulls alongside a rundown hotel and opens his door, leaving the engine running.

"Won't be a sec, hang on!" he yells back, in mid-hop out the door.

The last Wade sees of him is the hotel bar door swinging behind him. But true to his word, he's out again in less than a minute and Wade is relieved. They need fuel. They need coffee. Neither of them is especially hungry so they will keep driving. Norman isn't volunteering any information about his quick errand. Maybe he just had

- 150 -

to take a leak. He's been grousing about having some troubles with pissing and having to hold it.

"There's a great place up ahead in Kamloops for dinner. It'll be a late dinner, 8:30 or 9 p.m. but worth it, Wade, I tell ya!"

Norman's good mood is restored it seems and that's okay with Wade. It'll be their last dinner together on this trip and their last long haul of the season together. Make that, our last trucking together, anywhere, ever! He feels his spirits lift at the very thought of that.

Wade spots a handsome brick building with tall, pale pillars and wide steps and yells "Stop!" Norman complies with a hasty pullover since there is no traffic nearby. Wade jumps down from the truck and runs up the steps with his prepaid envelope, shoving it into the box for out of town mail. His spirits take another swift flight upwards.

One more stop at a busy little cafe for coffee to fill up their thermoses and they're on the road again. The coffee is excellent and Wade digs out Penny's triple-ginger gingersnaps for the occasion. The snow stops falling. Wade's world-view improves rapidly. Norman grumbled earlier about an accident that Wade had slept through near the hamlet of Parson that held them up nearly thirty minutes. Then he had to stop at the weigh scales back in Golden, another event Wade had slept through blissfully. Now as they leave the pretty mountain town bedecked with fresh snow, he is mock-complaining about a few fools in sport-utes who were accidents about to happen, zipping in and out of lanes with impunity, trusting their oversized tires and 4x4 traction on icy, slushy roads.

By Three Valley Gap, he has Carmina Burana back on the deck and cranked up. Wade dum-de-dums along with it, liking the complexity of all the parts, the joy, the menace, the loud, the soft, all of it. Maybe he'll get a CD for himself in Kamloops if there's time. He has three twenties tucked away that he hasn't yet spent on food.

Last Christmas, Gordon had given them a CD player he'd won at a store's grand opening draw. With his ever-present IPod, he claimed not to need one, which made Penny and Wade feel outdated on the spot. Although they had less than twenty CDs in their collection so far, Wade thought it was a good start. The new player sat beside his twenty-five year old stereo and lifetime collection of two hundred or so LPs and a relatively modern boom box and five hundred cassettes. Maybe he'd get the new Wailin' Jennys and Dixie Chicks for Penny this Christmas too. Once, he'd caught her dancing around the kitchen, harmonizing along with an early Chicks cassette while they dispatched a foul old fellow with verve and tuneful panache.

They'd both had a good laugh. Then they'd made love, in the early afternoon, another rare treat these days. They did stuff for each other that they hadn't done for years. He grinned, remembering how afterwards she'd dead-panned, 'Why, thank yuh, mister' and he'd bowed and said, 'Muh pleasure, ma'am.' With both kids off studying and Morris gone…, well, they might have more of those early afternoons and they could holler the house down if they felt like it.

But first things first. He has to take the remaining honey to the Kamloops drop-off first thing tomorrow and then head for home. He'll be home Sunday evening or Monday at the latest. Home! The envelope in Revelstoke's heritage post office will arrive after I do but this way I can blame the dump of early snow or the postal system in general and be in the clear with wee Penny. Hah!

Norman's good to keep on driving, caffeinated and in a fine frame of mind. Wade feels a little guilty at first but he knows Norman is likely making up for his surly mood and hogging the sleeper when Manon was with them. That was a long and tough stretch of driving, an all-nighter he won't forget for a long time. Wade sighs and drains his coffee mug, screws it back on his thermos and closes his eyes, just to rest them. He contemplates a hot dinner, splurging on a rare dinner out, and wishes he could follow that up with a shower, clean sheets and a good night's sleep. A decent dinner special in a cheap café would have to do.

"Hey, Wade? You mind if I drop in at that place up there by the lights?"

Norman is yelling in his ear. Wade shakes his head and then his neck, which seems to have developed a nasty crick in it. He's fallen asleep at a bad angle.

"Sorry?"

"The Sundowner, up there on the right, that big hotel and restaurant place for truckers. Got a friend I need to check in with. We're in Kamloops now, or close enough to it."

"Oh, sure, I mean, do you want me to pick you up later or what?"

Wade is trying not to sound surprised but this has come right out of the blue.

"We oughta stay overnight here, ya think?"

Norman puts out this request as a statement, almost politely, Wade can't help but notice.

"Yeah, well…we've never, you know, stayed in motels on these trips right? With the sleeper and the two of us, the point is keeping going round the clock, right? We're still running over a day late, close to two days. Right now we need to get this load to their Co-op depot and quick too," says Wade, checking his watch. "We're usually here by 4 o'clock on a Thursday, not eight p.m. on a Friday. I need you to help me unload at the Co-op if they're short-staffed."

"No, sorry, man, no can do this evening. This is pretty important."

"Well. Okay. I guess," says Wade, and Norman immediately begins grinding to a halt, pulling into the oversized parking lot.

"I'll come back for you in an hour and a half or so, right?" Wade gives him a quizzical look.

"Sure thing. We might be able to stay here, you know, if my friend can swing it," says Norman. "It's looking pretty dirty out there, weather-wise."

"I can't afford a room or anything. I'd just as soon keep driving for Prince George as be stuck here," Wade says. God damn you, Norman, he thinks, you're up to something again, I can sense it, and I won't have any part of it. And what I say goes too. I've got that part figured out now.

Norman doesn't say anything, casting his eyes down to examine the toes of his running shoes. Finally he shrugs and jumps out to walk toward the Sundowner. Wade notices that he has his duffel bag slung over his shoulder. Strange. Maybe this is the end of the line for the two of us after all…well, I'll swing by on my way north. So be it, whatever it is. Wade gets down from the passenger seat, does a wild swing of both arms and a groan-worthy attempt to touch his toes to loosen up before climbing up to drive.

Without a backward glance, he wheels the rig around and heads for the Co-op, turning off the music so he can concentrate on driving into the city. He has missed the turn-off to the railway area and the warehouse several times before, all in the proverbial blink of an eye.

Twenty minutes later, he is relieved to see the loading docks behind the Co-op are all clear. A wiry older man and a husky young fellow guide him as he backs the rig up to an open bay.

Forty minutes later, he wheels out again, heading back to the Sundowner. He is hungry but he doesn't really want to indulge Norman by spending the night. He has sixty bucks left and he'll suggest grabbing a couple of burgers on the way out of the city, just to keep on driving. Might even make it home by mid-afternoon Sunday, yes, have a nice Sunday dinner at home after an hour soaking his bones in the hottest bath possible. He'll call home, warn Penny. Oh shit oh shit oh shit! I told her I'd call. Long before this! Oh this is bad. I'll see if there's a public phone at this Sundowner place.

After slapping his own head, Wade settles down. He'll call tonight and man up. He relaxes, glad of the sparse traffic while navigating the downtown corridor out to the Trans-Canada and the Sundowner.

It was a relief to deal with the familiar Co-op people back there. But he was taken aback when they asked about their smoked salmon. They'd been expecting a good-sized shipment, fancy quality. The manager assured him of their order for a pallet's worth, as per a phone call on August 16th with a Mr. Norman Deville. He held out an ordering pad to show the handwritten notes he'd made during the call. Wade was blind-sided by this news and apologized, with feeling, and silently cursed Norman for once again dropping the ball on the solid Co-op orders, first the apples and now this. There are only twelve small bundles of salmon left in the truck and Wade wants the northern co-ops to try one each. He sold the ten remaining packs to Kamloops Co-op, trying not to take it personally when the manager kept muttering 'Well, I guess it's better than nothing. Got the Thanksgiving weekend hors d'oevres covered. Well, I guess that's better than nothing...'

He'd apologized several times over and swore it wouldn't happen again. He was given directions to the nearest post box only half a block away as he accepted their cheque for the new salmon product. The honey would be paid by direct deposit to the apiary as usual for established customers.

Wade leaps out of the truck with the motor still running and runs through the light sifting of fresh snow now coming down, icing sugar snow as Penny would call it, shoving the envelope into the exterior mail chute. He bounds back to the truck and swings himself up, his back feeling as limber as it ever is, these days.

Now, he wants to talk with Norman about this

salmon shipment detail. If he hadn't been up to his ass in alligators trying to sort out Morris' debts with Penny and then somehow getting two cuts of hay off and moving hives to and from the apiary for twenty-plus farmers and trucking grain for everybody and his dog for two months straight...but he should have made the time to handle the shipping orders on this trip. It isn't rocket science after all and if this is what happens the first time he lets someone else look after it, well, it won't happen again, that's all there is to it. But Norman had offered to take some of the load off his back. Truth be told, nobody else but Penny ever offers to do anything major for him, to be in his corner, have his back, call it what you will. He had handed over the Co-op contact list to Norman the week after the funeral. Gordon couldn't do it, had to leave right away, drive for seven hours to keep working as a vet's assistant in the Bulkley Valley all summer. Gwyneth worked at the university daycare all summer except for taking the plane home for the funeral. He hardly saw either of them when they came up for one short week at home for the last week of August. Couldn't expect the kids to wade into it all for him at a time like that either. He should have asked Penny but he didn't want to burden her with even more stuff. But she would have said yes or no, upfront, good and straight. But he was more than grateful to Norman for sorting out the orders on this trip, all the phone calls, all the confirmations, all the waiting around for call backs that he didn't have time for. But now as he thinks about it he should have made time, just like now, not calling Penny for days on end. She deserves better than that. I'll make it up to her, he promises himself, I will. Stop going over and over this stuff, just stop it! It's done!

When he parks at the Sundowner beside a long line-up of massive Kenworths and Macks, he notices the lot is nearly filled with pickups and that there are at least twenty big rigs besides his older and smaller International. The restaurant's brightly lit circular windows show a packed room, doing a busy trade. He walks in and hovers at the door, but there is no sign of Norman among the thirty tables. He heads for the bar.

The bar is at least five times the size of the restaurant. A live band is belting out a Waylon and Willie ripsnorter onstage at the far end of the cavernous room. He steps into the dimly lit space and lets his eyes adjust.

"Comin' through. Nobody move!"

A solidly built waiter trots in front of him with four wooden platters of sizzling steaks balanced on both tattooed arms. He looks more like a weight-lifter than a waiter to Wade, what with the shaved head, no neck, tight white T-shirt packed with triceps and biceps and even tighter blue jeans emphasizing massive thighs. A bit over the top, he thinks and keeps looking around. The place is nearly full already. 9:45 p.m.

Over the brightly lit bar area is a long banner announcing two steaks for the price of one. That explains the booming business with at least three other burly waiters moving at double-time with armloads of wooden platters. The aroma of fried mushrooms and onions and grilled steaks makes Wade's mouth water.

He moves forward and searches the tables in a methodical way for any sign of Norman. Then he hears familiar braying laughter. Norman stands behind the bar beside a tall black-haired woman. He spots Wade and waves him over.

"Wade! Got a friend I'd like you to meet, my man! My partner, Cicely, this is Wade. Wade from up north."

Norman is beaming from ear to ear.

Wade takes her outstretched hand and shakes it, trying to muster up a smile. She has a very cold hand and her oddly elongated dark brown eyes are even colder. She bares her teeth and nods.

"You're both very welcome to stay the night here," she says. "Norman tells me you two are kinda roughing it, driving that big old truck, catnaps along the way. I've got a couple of extra rooms so don't worry. It's on the house."

"And dinner's on me, man. Feel like a good steak?"

Wade caves. He is very hungry and he hasn't had a hot meal since he can't remember when on this drive. The burger and chips on the last ferry from Vancouver Island to the mainland maybe? And a real bed instead of the rank sweat-soaked foamy. What the hell! Prince George is an easy six hundred klicks, just a steady seven hours on good pavement up the north Thompson and the Yellowhead, then the final push through the Rockies up to the Peace. Six, maybe seven hours and we're home.

"Sounds good to me. Your offers are very generous. Thank you, both of you," he says and joins them at a round table in a nearby corner. He sags onto the chair, accepting the frosty mug of Big Tree ale brought to their table within seconds of being seated. Norman is still beaming.

"Cicely and I go back a long ways," he says. "Whatcha

think of the spread here? Seen much of it yet? Guess not, huh?"

"Uh, no, just got here. Just unloaded downtown and headed straight back. It's dark already," says Wade. "It seems like a thriving business though."

He nods at Cicely, who inclines her head gracefully in Wade's direction and sips on something clear in a tall glass with lots of ice.

"Would you believe forty rooms, this bar which is a solid goldmine, ditto for the restaurant and we got a casino in the works too? All the comforts of home for the knights of the road. Showers, clean sheets, truck wash, mechanics, good, cheap food. Excellent entertainment."

Norman winks at Cicely and waves one meaty hand in the air. "Not to mention, the best manager in the West in the person of Cicely here."

Cicely's eyes narrow even more and she takes another dainty sip of her drink. She is a very striking woman, tall and lean in a snug black jumpsuit with a silver and turquoise belt cinched around her waist. It's hard to tell exactly what age she is, though he thinks she could be anywhere between thirty-five and fifty-five. She looks like she could be Cher's sister, or at least her cousin, with the perfectly arched black eyebrows, country singer style big hair, plumped up lips and frosted coral talons. Norman looks very pleased with himself. An attractive business woman of a certain age to spend time with and free lodging tonight as well. Wade wonders how close this close friend is to Norman. He's never heard him mention her before.

A hulking waiter takes their orders and a second round of beer makes its way to their table. Wade dearly wants to take his boots off but resists the urge. The band takes a break, replaced by Shania Twain on the sound system.

Norman leans forward and talks to Cicely about their drive, in between long swigs of beer. Wade stays silent while Norman bellows on about the 'just awesome' scenery and 'these cornball little towns right outa the fifties, man' and ' these crazy characters we got for customers'.

Makes us sound like the Hardy Boys on a trucking adventure, for Pete's sake.

Cicely sits back and listens, eyebrows permanently arched, eyes unsmiling, baring her teeth at appropriate moments, the smooth planes of her face settled in an impassive, unreadable mask. Her narrow eyes continually rove around the bar. Occasionally she nods at someone who catches her glance.

Wade wants Norman to just shut up for a minute or two, so he can think. Or not think. He just wants to close his eyes for a second, let another wave of road-weariness climb all over him. He can't bring the salmon fiasco up now, in front of Cicely. Tomorrow, first thing, he'll talk business with him. But now he only wants to stretch out for an hour, to lie flat on his back with his boots off, enjoy a private snooze. First, eat. Then sleep. No, get good and clean before sleep. He excuses himself and goes to the john to wash his grimy hands and splash cold water on his face.

He's so damn tired all the time on this never-ending trip. Lord, I just want to get home in one piece, he tells himself, and do a few final chores and then hole up and rest my bones all winter. Maybe take up some kind of useful hobby while Penny sews her stuff. A hobby or a long-distance course of some kind. Feed my brain again, do something constructive, enjoy something different.

Yeah. To help me get over the fact that this work is no longer that much fun. I can't get away from it. I think I hate my life. I do. Not much fun at all, at all, he thinks. No sir. Living in that house, Morris' house, stuck there working and worrying non-stop, trying to comprehend the mess Morris' left behind instead of being free at last to do whatever it is he wants to do while he still has some time and energy left in him. Whoever that is, anymore.

He stares at himself, seeing the blue circles under his eyes, the greyness under his skin and the deepening grooves across his forehead. His face looks thinner, he thinks, squinting as he inspects his sideburns and hair for any more signs of rogue silver hairs. He finds one near his left temple and yanks it out along with a few of its black brethren. He tries to smile but he isn't in the mood to jolly himself out of whatever kind of funk this is.

When he figures he's been away long enough, he walks back to their table. The place is packed now, with not an empty table in sight. The band is back on its feet playing something zippy and instrumental that sounds like a cross between Waltzing Matilda and Freight Train. Perfect timing. Their steaks have just arrived.

Under Cicely's critical, unblinking eyes, they are each served an oversized wooden platter holding one large, foil-wrapped baked potato, fluffy and steaming, sixteen ounces of top-quality Black Angus sirloin steak, smothered in pan-fried button mushrooms and red onions, flanked by sautéed wisps of red, yellow and green peppers. They fall to it, heaping sour cream, butter, fresh chopped chives and crumbled bacon bits onto their potatoes.

"Gawd, we'll keep the heart and artery docs in business for years to come," groans Norman, finally pushing himself back from the table. "I'm slowing down. If I was younger, I'd top this off with apple pie and ice-cream."

"I'll have to put you on a diet, old man," says Cicely, with just the trace of a smile in her voice. "What did you think of that steak, Wade?"

"Honestly, it's one of the best I've ever eaten," he says. "Could have cut it with my fork."

She smiles a genuine smile this time and nods briskly.

"That's silver sirloin brand. It costs me more but you can see the word's out about the quality of the steaks we serve in here. Happy you liked it."

"I surely did."

"Norman, you are lucky to have a sensible friend like Wade here. He ate his vegetables and you need to finish yours," she says.

Norman lights up like a Christmas tree. He's sweet on her!

"Well, I hate to eat and run but I'm too much in need of a decent shower and a good sleep, myself," says Wade, turning down a third beer, excellent microbrew though it is, and the tempting dessert menu. Like Norman, he is stuffed to the gills.

Cicely reaches into her fringed black suede shoulder bag and pulls out a room key.

"Room 38. It's a nice, quiet one," she says, baring her teeth again.

"Thanks. Very much," says Wade. "See you at six for breakfast, Norman?"

"You betcha!"

*　　　*　　　*

By Monday afternoon, Penny has the Grade 11 and 12 students in her sewing Class double block, all young women except for one popular young man, at work on preliminary set and costume designs for 'Peace River or Bust!' Edie Maunsell, the drama teacher, has spent the first thirty minutes with them, going over the two-act play, scene by scene. Then she shows them slides of fashions worn by men, women and children in the 1930's, from Eaton's catalogue pages and from photographs collected by Aloysius Deacon. Penny grins when she hears this familiar name, even though she hadn't really enjoyed the content of his last visit. Aloysius is responsible for collecting most of the new and archival photographs for the Goodland Historical Society's forthcoming book. Then Edie shows slides from her own collection of photographs of her homesteading family.

One group of young girls stands in a row, grinning or scowling at the camera, all wearing plain little dresses made from fifty pound flour sacks. Edie points out her mother, one of the grinners in the line-up.

"If you look closely, you can spot the Five Roses logo," she says, pointing at the circle. "Even though they washed the material in the hottest water and put them out in the sun to fade and even rinsed them with bluing crystals. No bleach around for them."

"What did they use to dye the cotton with?" asks Josh. He had announced his plans for a design career in film and theatre at the start of the class. When Edie was introduced as the focus of the day's class, there'd been a theatrical throwing of his hands in the air.

"Finally!" he'd huffed. "We're moving on from pin cushions and prom dresses to stuff I'm actually interested in!"

Edie Maunsell beams at Josh. She is obviously familiar with him and not in the least deterred by the four silver rings in his ears or the studs and hoops in his eyebrows, nose and lips.

"Excellent question, Josh. Your next class in this double block will have your art teacher explaining exactly that process. We'd like this production to be as authentic as possible and yet the budget...," she pauses. "Our budget will also be true to Depression-era standards, with a bit of inflation allowed perhaps."

"What about asking people to loan us suits and dresses and stuff? My aunt has tons of great outfits that were passed down on her side of the family," pipes up Corinne. Her dark brown eyes, cupid lips and shining black bob of hair remind Penny of Mary Pickford in a 1920's flapper era film.

"They would be a terrific resource for you as designers and costume makers but with a five show run, three evenings and two matinees, priceless heirlooms will inevitably get wrecked. Remember, you'll have actors wearing lots of stage make-up and doing dance scenes. Sweating a lot, in other words. Some of them have three or four fast costume changes. We'll need plenty of Velcro, that great Canadian invention. Plus, I need you to think machine washable fabrics only for everything except the coats and hats, and those, thankfully, are from our permanent costume collection."

Penny feels her interest in the project quicken with Edie's enthusiasm followed by a pang as she realizes she won't be here to take part. She sighs but a hard little knot in her dissolves.

It's okay, she tells herself. Do what you can. Apply for a position after school today. Let the Board office know you want full or part-time work anywhere in the district. Wade will be home soon from this last trip. He can stay home and do the chores and I'll go out and make us some decent money. Morris isn't around to sneer at him for not being the breadwinner while Wade 'sits around the house'. As if either of us ever got to just sit around the house a whole lot in the first place! Okay, just do it today.

She thanks Edie and sets her over-sized posters of the basic wardrobe patterns on easels around the room at the student work tables. The task for the students is to define the details of the 1930's collars, sleeves, skirt and pant widths and lengths. They work on pages of mini-posters placed in front of them: men, women and children. Townsfolk, comfortably established or just getting by, homesteaders, a minister and a priest, school teachers, male and female, lots of children, town kids and farm kids. The sound of pencils and erasers and little exclamations of disgust or approval fill the air. She smiles at all their heads bent over their work.

Only one hefty young matron-in-training sulks and fumes, ignored by the other students at the same work table. Apparently she'd wanted to devote her entire year to making her own wedding trousseau as a directed studies course instead of following the curriculum with the rest of the class. Anna Schmidt had ruled against that. But Penny had also come across Anna's notes stating that Lana Sawatsky was an advanced seamstress with a goal of opening her own sewing and alterations business. Penny contemplates giving Lana some kind of attention and then decides it might be best to ignore her balkiness. Let her stew in her own bad-tempered juices for a while. Then she relents and asks Edie if there is a wedding in the script.

"Not yet, but what a good way to end the second act," Edie says. "The script, which is a work-in-progress as we speak, sort of wobbles off with a repeat of the theme song. But a wedding! Great idea, signifying hope and a new tomorrow, all that yadayada, followed by the show stopper tune with all the cast on stage, tossing bouquets of prairie crocuses at the crowd…, well now! I'm going to make an executive decision and run with that, thank you, Penny. Sure you don't want to stick around and be part of the action on this project?"

"I wish…it's wonderful, really! I'll see. It really does look like a lot of fun and well, let's just see how things work out for me here. Now, I think we have just the right person in this class to design the wedding party. Shall I get her underway?"

"Please do. Let's do four bridesmaids, four grooms-men, four flower girls, the ring bearer…oh, and make the bride and groom farm folk, not townspeople. No, wait! Make the bride a town girl and the groom a farmer. I can work that in with some fun business earlier on," says Edie, scribbling notes for herself as the director and dramaturge and contributing writer and interim stage manager.

"Oh. Oh. Oh! Thank you so much, I'll try my best to do a really, really good job!" says Lana, the future bride, her glum face now a study in pure joy.

Penny feels a rush of joy herself, for rising above student-teacher personality differences and for making a useful and creative suggestion at just the right time. If I'm not getting the message by now, I'm tone-deaf. I'm a good teacher and I should be doing this work because I really like it and I'm getting well-paid for it.

The bell rings a short ring to signify the break for the double block but most of the class of twenty-two keep on working. The bell rings again, three minutes later, and Frederic Murdoch strides in with a pile of paper under one arm and a large canvas bag as well.

"Hello, Ms. Toland, class," he announces, swinging his gaze from her to the students.

Was that a wink along with that languid smile?

He moves beside each work table, placing solid co-lour plates in front of them, talking all the while, a rap-id-fire explanation of colour and mood and receptors. He engages each group with their responses to the colours he'd placed in front of them. Penny silently applauds. Even Lana, Miss Trousseau, has deleted her pout entirely and is participating enthusiastically.

"Can you comment on using dyes for this project?" Penny asks during a lull.

To her amazement, he dives into the canvas bag and brings out plastic zip-lock bags containing black tea-bags, spruce needles, dried bear berries and dandelion roots, along with swatches of wool and cotton fabric dyed with each.

"In an ideal world," he says, "we'd go out collecting these and we'd experiment with indigenous materials like wild sage and kinnikinnick and pine cones and whatever else we could get our hands on. But we don't have the time for that for this project which is too bad. You'd do that if you were responsible for dressing the staff of a living museum exhibit, you know, where the people take on the roles of pioneers. You'd want absolute authenticity for something like that. But for this play, your very important role is to set the mood with five different sets, four of which need curtains, all of which need upward of thirty costumes. You've got eleven weeks to help get the play up on its feet, so what's the mood?"

"Bleak brown! Everybody's broke, right?"

"Farmer green? Sort of early back to the land happy times?"

"Blue because it's sort of an old-fashioned colour now."

"No, it's not! Where do you get that idea?"

"Yellow for the children's clothes because it's optimistic. The people who moved here wanted to improve the future life for their children, right? So let's put them in shades of yellow, flitting around like little sunbeams or whatever," Josh says.

Frederic applauds, laughing.

"Okay, sounds good to me! I think you're on the right track with that but get a proposal and sketches together and then have the director, Ms. Maunsell, agree to it. The director is like God, you know. Always gets the final say. Okay, we're still brainstorming here so what about the young farm women. We've got six of them to outfit for the play, am I right, Ms. Toland?"

White flash of teeth, dark eyebrows arching up over those amused blue eyes.

"Yes, that's right," she says. She checks the wardrobe chart in front of her, feeling self-conscious, willing herself not to allow any tell-tale heat to redden her face. She clears her throat briskly, keeping her eyes down as if studiously reading the chart.

"For the young women, I'd choose flower prints because they're still young and want to look pretty and not all worn-out with work and stuff," says the young Mary Pickford lookalike.

"Or pastels, if they had them back then? Two pinks, two light blues, two light greens, or maybe, do like Josh says for the kids, use one colour, say pink or rose, whatever, but use different shades, darker, medium, pale, or as prints, that's pretty, two for each of them. That way, if you're way back in the audience, when you see the young women dancing, it'll be, like, obvious it's them. You'd get it right away," another student says, the one that Penny notices is always sketching, her hand flashing confidently over her sketchbook.

Frederic gives this suggestion a thumbs-up, nodding approvingly. And then they are all off and running, with Frederic skilfully bringing them back on topic, staying focused on the task at hand. Josh suggests using aprons for the women's workdays and hats and shawls for church events, over the same dresses.

"It would save wardrobe money, right? Use the basic dress but add to it. When in doubt, accessorize, my Mom says," Josh tosses out, miming the adjusting of a hat.

All too soon, the final bell rings. Penny thanks Frederic before he ambles out and then she quickly assigns each of them two sketches for homework.

She shakes her head to clear away the black thought of wishing Anna Schmidt a complicated recovery, one that would require bed rest for the next eleven weeks. She hasn't taught teenagers before in a formal school situation except for one week as an experiment when she was still in university, which hardly counted since she was an observer and assistant, not planning and teaching classes. The Goodland Elementary Christmas concerts didn't really count as a large-scale creative challenge. With cute kids and three-quarters of the crowd composed of their close relatives, any song and dance performed by each grade was a guaranteed hit. But here she was in a high school, enjoying it all very much. Not to mention the little frisson of a smart, creative and very fetching art teacher wandering around the same halls.

Penny gives herself the mental equivalent of a bop on the head. She gathers up her papers and Anna Schmidt's lesson plan book. Time to face the Grade Nine foods class, the last class before lunch. Into the lion's den marches Ms. Toland.

I know I went back outside to get my shaving gear and some clean clothes... Then I started rummaging around in the sleeper, trying to find my book. Thought I heard voices then but it was just a couple guys walking from their trucks, heading to the bar.

Next thing I knew someone was right in my cab and I went, oh hell, here we go again, you know? Somebody wanting a ride or something worse, like thieving. But it was Norman and I don't know who jumped most, me or him.

He said he was getting some stuff he'd forgotten too. And was I sure I didn't want some entertainment? You could hear this guy leer in the dark.

I asked what he was on about.

Entertainment.

What, exactly?

The special rooms, is what he said.

But I begged off, wanting a hot shower more than anything in the world at that moment. I found my room, on the 3rd floor, nice big window looking right into a thick stand of spruce trees, I remember that... I proceeded to have about half an hour under pelting hot water, one of those oversized multi-speed shower head units, you know? Unknotting my neck and shoulders, lambasting my spine.

I wasn't tired after that, not tired enough to sleep. I needed to walk around after all that sitting, tensed up, watching for the ditch or the cliffs in Rogers Pass or for headlights coming straight at us. I put on my change of clean clothes and felt normal again, well-rested, well-fed, clean and shiny.

So I started down the hotel hallways and walked three long floors, thinking I might just do that a couple more times, keep stretching my legs. And then I came to a heavy steel door on the bottom floor, right beside the ice machine. Just curious, you know?

So I pushed it open into another corridor but it locked behind me. So I carried on, went into another corridor, got to the end of that, went through another heavy door which opened into a busy, noisy lobby sort of room, filled with men. There were more of the waiter-bouncer types parked in front of other doors and a buzzer went off as the door I came through clanged behind me.

The closest bouncer-type came over but I decided, don't ask me why, to just step forward smartly and pretend it wasn't me who came through and set off the alarm. It was so packed in there that it was easy enough to casually infiltrate a circle of guys standing around talking. The bouncer banged at the door, which had no doorknob on this side, I noticed, too late.

He asked a couple of nearby guys something I couldn't hear in the hub-bub. I just kept my head down and kept moving into the crowd. A cocktail waitress dressed in a cigarette girl outfit, you know the fishnet stockings, roller skates, white apron, the little French maid look? Anyway, she scooted around our circle with a platter of tequila shooters, salt shakers and limes so we all drank up. I didn't want the strong booze but I didn't want to look out of place.

Then another buzzer gave a couple of short blasts

and the room erupted in cheers and yahooing before settling down. Each of the three bouncer types made an announcement about the next hour behind the door they were each guarding.

"Amazon Girls, total nudity, three college girls with no time for men until…guess what? And who will be the lucky gentlemen they'll pick out here tonight? Held over by popular demand!"

"No holds barred. No TV showmanship. It's Deranged Dino from Drumheller taking on Big Bill Billabong, the Aussie nut-case gladiator, in a grudge match to unconsciousness or worse. Guaranteed!"

"Special tastes for special gentlemen. Fur and feathers will fly! You know who you are and what you like to watch, gentlemen. A very special show tonight for you all."

I couldn't see any sign of Norman and I didn't want to go into any of their special entertainment rooms. Sicko stuff if you ask me. Yeah, it's pretty much plastered everywhere on the Internet and TV and all that crap but I think this was hardcore stuff. I don't go for any of it, absolutely no way. So I started heading for the other end of the room while all these other guys were lining up for their vice of choice. I told the beefy guy at the far door I wanted to find my buddy first and he checked my door key and nodded. Let me out without another word.

Bang, there I was outside, at the bottom of a long flight of steps, dark as a dungeon, and not a clue which end of the place I'd gotten myself to. It was cold, really cold and I didn't have my coat on. So I started walking around the building, thinking I would end up at the right door if I just kept going and that's exactly what I did.

I went back to Room 38 and realized I just didn't want to stay there. The place creeped me out. So I grabbed my coat and my kit and went back down to the bar to see if Norman was still hanging around. And there he was, still sitting at the table we'd had our steaks on. Cicely was behind the bar, hands flying, mixing fancy drinks. He looked happy to see me, that big monkey face of his always lit up like a lamp.

He stuck his arm up for a round of beer before I could stop him and then I thought, what the heck.

Why are we getting the royal treatment at this joint? I wanted to know.

Because I'm her silent partner, man, he crowed. This establishment is my nest-egg. Me and Cicely are partners. She manages it and does a super job, didn't I think?

My jaw must have dropped but now something fell into place and made sense. He'd even introduced her to me as his partner and all along I'd thought he was telling her that I was his business partner. I'd taken offence to that, actually, but I didn't want to cause a fuss by splitting hairs in front of her.

I knocked back the beer and told him I was going to hit the sack and that I'd had all the entertainment I could stand.

That Norman. I'd never talked money with him so I had no idea where he was sinking his savings or even if he had any. All I knew of him was that he'd worked in the oil-patch until he got sick of the work and the isolation and that he worked at driving for me and other people too, part-time odd-jobbing. I didn't figure him for a wealthy businessman type, that's for sure. What I mean with Norman was that, until now, he was completely silent about what he did with his life or money. It was none of my business to pry either. People either volunteer their business like it's no big deal or they treat their money like it's a deep mysterious secret.

There's lots of ex-Yanks in Canada who are from fairly wealthy families you know, but Norman never mentioned his family to me. Very private, that guy. Full of surprises. I know he's got a social insurance number for Canada but then lots do, and they hang onto their U.S. citizenship. Figure they've got the best of both worlds and they do because we're too polite to boot them out.

Now Norman is different again. He's no social worker or Quaker or conscientious objector kind of man. He could be a working-class guy from a rough and tumble kind of family or he could be a rebel escaped and slumming on a trust fund from a wealthier type of family. An opera-lover from New York City. Could be from some European background, Italian, Greek, maybe. Deville? French is very possible, lots migrating down from Quebec to the States for years. Some of those folks changed their names when they went to the States, or had their names changed for them by pencil-pushers. The old melting pot boiling everyone down to Coke-swilling, weenie-eating, red-blooded Americans.

Norman Deville. Somewhere in his early fifties, I think.

I hired him because I didn't trust anyone under thirty to drive my truck. And he has his airbrakes licence.

We've done four of these long trips together. One of us drives while the other sleeps or we just listen to music and go our own separate ways, in our heads. It suited us both just fine. Very easy to deal with someone who's good at the actual work and makes few demands of a person. Other than getting used to his bad ear and his bellowing and his loud music which I happen to like, by the way. It always made me feel like I was traveling in Hungary or Italy or Spain, yeah, someplace more hot-blooded with the kind of operas he liked.

I miss him, in a way. I mean, I miss the first guy I knew, the easy-going, wise-cracking, what you see is what you get kind of Norman I knew during those first road trips.

When did I know, for sure? I think…I didn't want to admit to myself what I was pretty sure was happening for too long. There hadn't been any sign of this in the first four trips because it was very straight-ahead. Delivery and pick-ups at the Co-ops in each of those places. But this time, with all the changes and the Co-ops being dropped except for the ones in Cranbrook and Kamloops…well, that first drop, at that little island off the Coast? That was when he started holding things up and getting me stoned on hash brownies and laughing at me for being uptight about the ferry schedules and not giving me the cheque which was mine, by rights… well, I just didn't want to look at him straight during that island stop. I kept waiting for things to return to normal and they never did.

Then that biker gang and the potatoes and all, well, that just had to be a front for a shady operation. Quality hydroponic weed, underground meth lab, who knows? Even this naive hick from the north country knew enough to get the hell out of there as fast as I could. Norman was strange about that abused woman I hid in the truck, too. A good, hardworking gal in the wrong place at the wrong time. He had no pity at all, not an ounce and he'd always been kind of a puppy around women before then. Always kind of shy and goofy and eager.

I think now that he was worried about what she might know about the drug operation. I don't think he understood that she'd been kidnapped. Or if he figured it out as quick as I did, he'd know there could be kidnapping and rape charges there. But she didn't trust she'd be safe or protected if she pressed charges, I don't think. But Norman helped get us out of that place, stayed calm with those rifle-packing guards. He was very cool-headed, give him credit for that.

I'm such a trusting fool, such an idiot. I just go along with things, always have, easier than bucking the tide, arguing, but now, this…

I passed out cold in the sleeper. I didn't want to go back to that room and I had my own sleeping bag. I never knew what hit me. It had to be something in the beer, I figure, something without taste.

Roofies? You could be dead-on but I thought they lasted a lot longer. I can't remember all of it…okay, clearly now, I have myself waking up in the sleeper and it's damn cold. More fresh snow falling outside. I've got my boots off but I still have my clothes on, and I'm halfway into my sleeping bag. The cab is locked. So I must have gotten myself out there and then passed out.

My watch said 3:20 a.m. I had a dry mouth and I needed to pee or puke or both, really badly. I finally got my head on straight and my boots back on and started getting up to head out for some relief. That's when I heard the shuffling in the load behind me. Men's voices, quiet. I just got mad then.

I groped around behind the driver's seat for a big crescent wrench I keep stashed there and I twisted the interior light out of its socket so it wouldn't light up when I opened the door. I crept out, shivering like a dog, and tiptoed my way to the back where I could see a truck parked right behind me. I ducked under the trailer and got myself down to where the action was and then I stopped and listened. There were two of them and Norman. They were moving the load around and I could hear Norman giving orders about where to put stuff.

Then I made the mistake of being a stupid, polite hick of a Canuck again and stepped out to ask just what was going on here. The two strangers looked like the waiters, you know, like bouncers and one of them didn't even stop turning with a package in his hand. He just swung a huge fist, nailed me right on the chin. I remember banging back and bashing my head on the truck and that's all until coming to in the room with Norman and Cicely.

I started to puke and my head felt like it was splitting open. I couldn't breathe at all. I started to gag and that's when Norman jumped up and yanked the duct tape they'd covered my mouth with. I could have drowned in my own vomit if they'd just tossed me in the ditch somewhere.

When that Cicely saw I was truly awake, she snapped at him to 'deal with it' and turned on her heel, leaving him with me. He looked bad, I'll give him that, like a dog caught killing chickens the second time. He tried to speak a couple of times, putting those big paws of his out in the air between us as if he could make a shape out of what he'd been up to behind my back. I was tied to a chair in there, did I say that?

He untied me and took me outside, still not saying a word. It was a frozen alley, behind the truck wash and the garage wing of this place. I could hear somebody spraying down their rig and I could see the blue sparks of someone welding in a garage bay. Otherwise there was nothing except flat plateau rolling away from there. It was getting light out but the snow was still coming down.

Norman gave me my crescent wrench and the truck keys as I was rubbing the circulation back into my arms and stomping my feet. He just gave me a long, steady look and whispered for me to whack him. I stared at him, thinking I hadn't heard right.

He said he was sorry, that I didn't deserve this and that he wanted me to just get the hell out of there after I hit him. 'It's you or me, man, she's hard as nails and I can't do you so you'd better just give me a tap with that and be on your way and be mighty quick about it'.

I think I tried to talk but I couldn't, somehow. My mouth just drooled and I felt sick. I leaned against the cement wall and kept on my feet.

Today, I would ask him what kind of drugs he was hauling in my truck. Just what was worth the big bucks and the risk of prison for smuggling and out-and-out drug trafficking big payloads. I'd ask exactly what it was in the space the apples should have been and who those customers were that we'd had in B.C.

I mean, I'm not completely stupid, not anymore, anyway. This was unreal, the stuff that happened in suspense novels and that you hear broadcast on the news about someone else getting a truck across the U.S. border. This was never a reality in my kind of life.

But I just hung on to the outside wall in the cold, shaking and swaying on my feet. Then I puked everything up, landing on my knees in the gravel, feeling as weak as a kitten. He grabbed the crescent wrench where I'd dropped it and gave it to me and then he turned around. I spat and hauled myself up and, I still can't believe I did this, I tapped him on the back of his head. Not too hard but still, he buckled to his knees and toppled over.

I dropped the wrench. I remember I fell down on my knees again and I felt for a pulse in his neck. He groaned and his eyelids fluttered and I knew it was probably okay. So I grabbed my wrench and staggered off to my truck, not looking left or right, just concentrating on keeping my feet moving without falling down. It took a hundred years, felt like I was running through wet cement, but I got to it and I…was I looking for my shaving gear then?

Did I go inside the truck for…, no, I did that.

I said that already.

I drove away from that place and I left Norman there.

I just left him there.

*   *   *

There is a new notice up on the community bulletin board outside the Goodland Co-op and Penny stops to read it. Standing in front of it, her eyes swim in and out of focus, the map and dense grey text meaningless. She grips her envelopes and grocery flyers in one hand and keeps her face still. She can feel some eyes upon her.

There is nothing from him. Nothing. She has the final post-dated cheques for all eight of the horses she's boarding over the winter though. She hadn't been entirely sure about the character of the man who owned the three palominos. He was a big talker, a showboat with flashy horses he couldn't be bothered to look after himself. Now she'd find out if the cheques were any good, especially his, Mr. All Hat No Cows. There was always that. Then she has the Credit Union statement from September and a second notice yellow slip, not the final pink one, the baler repair bill from the John Deere dealership, and a Saskatchewan elevator postcard from Gordon.

"Dear Ma & Pa Kettle, How's life? Our Large Animal class went on a field trip to a horrible place where they're still keeping mares pregnant and tied up to collect their urine for menopause pills. The foals are shipped off for zoo food and a few are rescued. Five of us, four women and macho me, walked out halfway through the big tour. Prof seemed very pleased with us. Pork shipping conditions and "humane" cattle feedlot tour tomorrow. Your future SPCA investigator and vegetarian vet, Gordon xoxo"

Penny grins, kisses the stamp on the postcard, then collects her thoughts and focuses on the bulletin board. The sign refers to new road construction, something about joining the new Snoose Creek gas field with the highway. `Sand and gravel wanted`. She peers at the fine print under the grey map of the township. There is the field, on Sections 300, 301 and 302 and there, running right alongside their own #303 quarter-section was the proposed new road. That would chop the regular winding route to the refinery to less than a quarter of the distance. Time equals Money.

She frowns, thinking it over. At least it won't pass right by her kitchen window. That quarter-section is marginally productive grey-wooded soil, fairly flat, now producing only one thin crop of alfalfa annually. But, as Gordon said, the alfalfa was pumping nitrogen back into the land, improving it, and the scant hay crop could be considered a bonus. The road allowance was fenced by a rickety two strands of barb-wire on their side, and they only ever used the allowance for moving their farm machinery.

The Lafleurs, neighbours on the other half-section, had their land ploughed up in summer fallow this year and it had never been fenced. They usually raised a stunted crop of barley on it but the foxtail and blue burrs and other weeds had gained too much of a foothold there. Wade had been relieved this spring when they'd spent the time and money ploughing it all under and then cultivating it again to curb the weed crop. He'd suspected old Lafleur's grandson, Roger Lemieux, had taken over and had set about properly farming the place. Even the home place was looking much more spruced up.

Penny surreptitiously writes down the phone number and contract code from the poster on the back of the horse payment envelope and then drives home in the relentless drizzling rain with a plan taking shape. By the time she turns down their side road, she has it worked out. She steps on the gas and keeps it floored until she has to stomp on the brakes in front of their big pole gate.

Casey races around her, yipping in ecstasy, getting in the way, kneeling and grinning, bowing and weaving. He knows something exciting is up. That much is plain to see as Penny runs up the front steps and goes straight to the phone without taking off her coat.

They can meet with her on Thursday morning and she will take them straight down the road allowance to where Little Deer Creek peters out and the slumping banks of sand and gravel make cultivation impossible. The stuff is right there, right beside their proposed new road. If she doesn't take them to that immense pile on their side, Old Ferdinand Lafleur would likely hear about it soon enough. Then he would usher them to the lesser mound still available and just as easily accessible across the road allowance on his own half-section. The contractor might use up both, in fact, but Penny wants first dibs at least.

She needs time during this weekend to plan three days worth of home economics lessons and she counts on not being called in for a fourth day, next Thursday. The road project is too valuable to pass on, a once in a lifetime thing. And it isn't as if it is good arable or even grazing land. It is better than that. It's interesting land, at least to Penny's way of looking at it. That pile of rocks showed where an even more ancient river than the Muddy had left behind its bed, occupied only seasonally now by Little Deer Creek. It is now useful land, as well as ancient and interesting terrain, if there is sufficient quality and quantity of sand and gravel.

It just might save the ranch from ruin, from the mistakes made by Morris.

Penny flies at the outdoor chores, promising Mister Bojangles his return to the harem in just three or four more days, watering, feeding, collecting the eggs laid after her first early morning search, scratching the affectionate weaner pigs between their shoulder blades for sentimental reasons, refraining from telling them their days on earth numbered less than a fortnight.

She doesn't think Wade will mind about that scrubby piece of land being used for a gravel pit, as far away from the house as it is possible to be and still be on the Toland ranch. She's never acted on her own like this before. Besides, Wade would surely be back long before Thursday and they can go out together with the highways contractor if she isn't needed for teaching. That thought cheers her up. Morris had made all the big decisions about buying and selling machinery but even he had never done much with the land. He'd worked with what he'd been left and, Penny is grimly certain, Morris hadn't been left with a whopping pile of debts by Gavin and Amelia Toland either.

Morris rotated nearly half the arable land to hay crops, the rest to oats and that combination had worked well with increasing the cattle herd size. If the weather co-operated, it made for a self-sustaining operation and it was somewhat less weather-dependent than making a go of it with only cereal grains. But Morris could never be described as an innovative rancher. Penny sometimes wished she had majored in agriculture instead of home economics.

Or, closer to the truth, she wishes that Wade had gone to university and studied agriculture instead of dropping out after one year of general sciences the year his mother died. He'd just wanted to try it out, he'd told her, see if he leaned toward anything in particular and he was more partial to biology than physics. His mind hadn't been firmly set on a career goal.

Morris didn't really want Wade away from the land in the first place but he gave in to Margaret Rose who insisted on sending him on for more education. His mother had fought two different kinds of cancer for seven years, from when Wade was fourteen until he turned twenty-one. Penny can only imagine what that fact did to Wade's concentration and goal-setting and academic success. How would Gwyneth and Gordon have coped in his shoes?

He rarely complains but really, he didn't get a fair shake at the start and now, when he might have had the time and opportunity to pursue his own education or even travel, like we used to imagine doing at some point in our lives together, we are trapped in this monumental financial mess.

Stop it, she tells herself. Things are starting to look up. Stay positive. It has to work. It just has to.

*　　　*　　　*

Penny Toland and the new teacher. That Art Guy. That's what the old farts and aging tarts down at the post office were gossiping about this Tuesday afternoon. Hazel can hardly wait to tell her.

"They said you were too good-looking a woman to be left out there all by your lonesome the way you are with Wade gone half the time," Hazel says. "They heard that new art teacher took his classes out to dig clay from your place. 'Sure wouldn't mind finding clay in those shapely little banks myself.' That's what Mort Granger said. Well, it was funnier the way he said it."

Penny stands like a stone. Hazel finally registers her silence but then she repeats her favourite maxim: "Oh come on, Penny. Where's your sense of ha ha? You know how it is, if you haven't heard a good rumour by noon, start one of your own."

I can't think of anything smart or nonchalant to say, to dismiss it all as beneath any sort of mention. Those raisin eyes of Hazel's are glued to my face, that oyster mouth is positively wet with anticipation. Penny has the strongest urge to belt her in the chops but she can't. I've got to sigh and roll my eyes, act above it all. People watch teachers like hawks watch a hen house. Teachers in small communities are fair game. Everyone knows which ones drink too much, who is shacked up with whom, whose kids are holy terrors themselves, the ones who aren't terribly bright, who are mean-spirited, arrogant and worse, who don't even actually like kids, and finally, thankfully, most people are grateful for those who are talented, hardworking, fair-minded and above all, kind to their children and compassionate with struggling parents.

"Penny?"

"Yeah?"

"Don't you worry. I can see I should have kept my big mouth shut. I don't know what I was thinking to pass on silly stuff like that. I should know better after teaching all these years myself. You know that's what I like about you, you never gossip and I should remind myself of that. Those old people have nothing better to do…"

Hazel stumbles and stops. She turns to face Penny, her plump face contorted into an expression of remorse so fervent it nearly makes Penny laugh out loud. Penny supposes she should say something, belittle the situation in some way. Be a good sport. Have a laugh at her own expense. No. She isn't going to let Hazel off the hook like that.

"It's an awful kind of character assassination, some gossip is," Penny says, softly, firmly, locking her eyes onto Hazel's. "Can you imagine what my children or Wade would feel like if they ever, ever overheard something like that?"

Hazel hangs her curly strawberry blonde head.

"I'll call Mort Granger and tell him to grow up and just…just shut up," says Hazel, who could do no such thing.

"Don't bother. It will have more impact coming from me," says Penny, leaving Hazel standing outside the Co-op. She wouldn't bother phoning him either. It would only fuel the flames. She could just hear Mort's nasal croak declaring to his cronies that she was madder than a wet hen and where there's smoke, there must be fire and every other silly cliché he could think of. Then they'd all have a good laugh, sitting on the Co-op bench like a bunch of croaking vultures dissecting everyone else's private business.

She drives home, fuming, furious with them all and angrier still at Wade. No phone call, no explanation as to why he's two days later than he should be. No cheque in today's mail. No excuses of his will suffice. He is being disobedient to Papa and she has seen this many times before. It is her life his immature stupidity affects. She isn't Morris and she isn't putting up with this crap any more. He is an adult, a grown-up, pushing forty-five for Pete's sake!

So what would she do about it?

What could she do about it?

Wait. Just wait.

And hope that everything is all right. Try not to think of breakdowns.

Or the nasty blizzard in south-eastern B.C., right smack on his route, all over the weather news.

Wait.

Wait and hope.

Crying is not going to help.

Won't help a damn thing so stop it, just stop it!

*   *   *

Okay, I remember, I drove... I was on my own but I was driving in a regular blizzard and it took forever to get to Prince George. Twelve hours. Fuelled up, found a coffee shop. Had to stay awake. Felt so shaky. Ate a dry bagel. Toasted. I remember that.

I went back to the truck. Crawled into the sleeper

for a nap and just conked out. I mean, how much sleep had I had the night before? I don't know anymore. All I know is that I felt awful and dog-tired.

After that? Woke up but it was dark again. Slept twelve and a half hours, the whole day through, and it was very, very cold in that cab. I was hungry and stiff all over. Stumbled into the world and followed the flashing lights down the street to a cabaret, the Cowpunk Cabaret. Me, thirsty, hungry, you name it. Nothing unusual, nothing to distinguish me from the rest of the clientele.

I used the public phone, I tried, I know that much. I tried about nine times that evening but she wasn't home. I couldn't figure out why and then I asked the bartender and found out it was Saturday. Maybe she was in town at some Farmers Market or something. Why wouldn't she put the answering machine on? Forgot, I guess. Not like her at all to forget, especially with the kids away. Or maybe she went out to do some visiting, who knows? Anyway, I relaxed about that. Figured if she wasn't home, maybe they were having a dinner or choir fundraiser up at the Hall or something.

Surf and turf special on the sign outside the Cowpunk Cabaret. Did I mention that's why I went there? For the cheap food, not the booze or scouting around for available ladies.

I got a small table next to the stage right beside the speaker. Not a prime spot, you might say. Which is why it was the only table left. Nobody else wanted to get their brains blasted out next to those speakers. But they had a $6.99 steak sandwich special, even cheaper than the surf and turf, so I stayed.

You might not think much of me now.

Well, I believe I fell in love.

They were an all female rockabilly band. The Sireens. Drums, mandolin, banjo, stand-up bass, dobro, lead guitar, two fiddles, guitars. Five of the most lovely, talented musicians you could ever set eyes on, amazing.

Well, there I was with eyes as big as saucers and I became their running gag of the evening, you know, the lonesome cowboy off the trail?

Their eye contact would have singed the chest hairs off every able-bodied male in the first five rows. Did I mind being picked on? Not a chance.

First, second and last breaks of the evening they came on down to my table and introduced themselves. Camille, Tracee, Annie, Gloria and Bonnie. By the last break, Annie pretty much had a song written for me. 'The Lonesome Trucker's Lament' or something. Such pretty harmonies, pure bluegrass. They were real musicians, this band, the same material as Allison Kraus and Union Station, the same tight harmonies. Great. Anyway, they'd been playing together for eight years and didn't tour much because some of them had little kids and family stuff and responsibilities, you know how it goes...so Smithers was their home base and Prince George and Prince Rupert were about as far as they strayed from home base.

That Annie! And Bonnie was her sister. They had smiles that would melt your spine away. Voices like angels, could harmonize with each other like...like sisters I guess. They could all play any instrument on the stage except Tracee. She stuck to the drums. Gorgeous spiky silver hair. Amazon woman, tall as myself with smooth but definite arm muscles, a show-stopper.

Why I guess the point is that they liked me and I liked them all and I liked them too much to be a jerk, you know? Sure, I wished I was single and young and up for any kind of good time hi-jinks. But nah, it was just plain fun.

Stayed up partying with them, doing the butterfly and the two-and four-handed schottische, and singing, all of us just singing our heads off until 4:00 a.m. I had to leave and it wasn't easy.

'Just one more song,' they'd wheedle and away we'd go. Until I snuck away to the bathroom and then headed for the door. Made it to the truck, stuck in my ear-plugs and bang, I was down and out like a light.

*   *   *

Penny arranges to meet him at the Goodland Co-op at 10:00 a.m. and then have him follow her to the site. He wasn't familiar with this part of the country, he'd said on the phone. She zigzags south and east until she stops at the grassy road allowance alongside the north end of the Toland property.

"Here's where you'd have access," she says. "It's pretty hard-packed because both neighbours have used it for years, hauling haying equipment and whatnot between fields."

Guy Chevrier kicks at the ground, nodding. She now knows they want to complete the road in the next two months, six weeks if possible. The ground would only get more frozen in the following two months so this roadbed could manage the heavy trucks. No sloughs or springs to deal with. He grunts approvingly.

"Shall we head down? It's just past that pine bluff."

"Fine with me," he says. He jumps into his company truck.

It is a raw, blustery day and his ears and nose are reddened. He looks tired and grumpy, possibly hungover, judging by the pale complexion and dark circles under his hang-dog eyes. He'd said all of eight words to her so far. Penny shivers and wishes she had worn her longer winter coat even if it is too dressy. Her nose is running and she blows it hard in the privacy of her own car. Then she grabs her keys and jumps into Guy Chevrier's Dodge Ram. Her Dodge Dart doesn't have high enough clearance for this stretch of driving.

The truck heater is blasting out good heat and she sighs, grateful for the warmth even if the interior smells a little sour, like old socks or something. He drives slowly down the road allowance until the bend and then she hops out to open the gate she had just made on Sunday, for exactly this purpose.

It had been a practical excuse that afternoon, telling Frederic that she had to leave him and the eight students at their clay-digging but if they wanted to stop by for hot cocoa afterward they were more than welcome. She packed the wire-stretcher, hammer, tin snips, collapsible hand saw, hatchet, fencing staples and extra wire into saddle-bags and rode Maggie May up to this spot, only twenty minutes from the diggers. There was an old stack of undersized fence posts cached near the corner of the field and she dragged four of them back to the spot by herself, on foot, as it was too cumbersome to attempt to use Maggie May for the task.

She'd never made a new gate before though she

had plenty of experience mending old ones. For now, she just wanted something that would hold up and do the job. She planned on coming back to improve it, or to ask Wade if he would take a look at it, if the road contract actually went through. But she is pleased now when she sees the wire and pole contraption still upright, taut, not sagging. She swings it open wide and motions the truck through.

"Over here. These banks," she points.

Guy squints at the high sage and grass-covered banks and grabs a spade from the back of his truck. Penny leaves him alone while he shovels and scrapes at the thin topsoil, then takes out a tape measure and repeats this same procedure in different spots, making notes in a small book. Penny wishes she had brought along a thermos of coffee. The north wind is picking up and there is a biting cold edge to it.

She starts walking up to the pine bluffs for their shelter. Under the first big pine she gets to she finds part of a small animal's skeleton she doesn't recognize. She carefully picks up the skull and wraps it in her spare handkerchief. Gordon can identify it when he comes home.

She can see Guy is still working down at the gravel site. He is a short, compact sort of man, with an athletic build. Penny sizes him up from a safe distance. Divorced, she'd bet money on it. Those sad hound dog eyes and no hint of a smile, a morose sort, all business, digging away steadily, a determined man. He wouldn't still be here if it isn't worthwhile, she reasons.

She walks around under the creaking pines and thinks she hears horses. She knows they would shelter under these old trees in bad weather but her bunch shouldn't be over here on this quarter. There is no watering hole on it for them and nothing but sparse alfalfa stubble in the fields. She rarely comes here because it is such flat, unappealing land to ride on with this small pine bluff about the only scenic relief to be found. But she hears the whickering again.

Penny looks up at the swaying treetops, turning in a circle and then stopping, feeling a little dizzy, unwell. It's the barometric pressure, she thinks, the low pressure storm front coming in, the weather changing. Even her head feels achy. A raven makes funny clunking and clicking sounds and she knows it has spotted her even if she can't see it. Maybe the raven has taken up horse noises as part of its vocal repertoire, the grand imitator that it is. Trickster bird.

She looks down at the dry mossy ground and then she sees them. Their rib cages and large bones, green with age, scattered here and there. Coyotes and wolves would have had a banquet.

Those large, long skulls are unmistakable. She counts nine of them before heading back down to the truck where Guy is just putting the spade and a half-filled gunny sack in the back. He nods at her return and gives a thumbs up to the banks.

"Looks good, real good," he says. "I've got one other place to check but with the road running right along here, well, we couldn't do much better. Pretty big deposit too."

Penny smiles a cautious kind of smile, not showing her teeth. She doesn't want to look too eager and she has a bit more digging to do herself about what the going rate is for square yards of gravel. She has to phone a few places and make sure she isn't going to be taken advantage of, price-wise.

Guy is almost chatty, certainly in better spirits, on the drive back up to her car, asking about the farm history. She gives him a brief history of Gavin and Amelia Toland and William and Grace Good and by then they are back to her car. She doesn't have time to tell him about Margaret Rose Good and Morris Toland and she probably would have been fairly terse about them if she had. She does not want to appear desperate. Or nowhere near bankrupt. Her left eye has, mercifully, stopped its involuntary twitching after her first day of the home economics subbing job in town.

She doesn't tell him about the horse graveyard she has just found and she never would but she will ask Wade when he gets home if he knows anything. It is a peaceful place, strangely enough, beneath those big old trees.

Then, as she is swaying down the road heading home, she remembers a story Wade told her a long time ago.

Amelia Toland loved horses but when they were too old or too sick to pull the ploughs and wagons, she and Soren Svenstrom, the hired man, would ride over to the pine bluff, leading the old timer. She would give the horse one last feed of oats under the pines, with their riding horses tied up a good distance away. She would let it chew its last oats on this earth and then she would signal to Soren to shoot it with a .303, one accurate shot behind a trusting ear. Then she would take the rope off its neck, mourn the faithful, fallen horse and slowly ride back home with Soren.

Grandpa Gavin wouldn't do it, couldn't shoot any-thing apparently, after the war, and Amelia wouldn't let just anyone shoot her beloved horses so she talked Soren into it. He would do anything she asked of him. There was Goodland gossip about that as well, of course.

Soren worked for the Tolands from 1947 until 1970, when Wade's grandmother died. Penny recalls Wade's face and voice darkening as he told her the next part.

The week after Amelia's funeral, Morris ordered Soren to shoot Amelia's saddle horse, a fine eight year old gelding with Morgan blood, the horse that had kicked Morris when he was being mean to it. When Soren objected, Morris said he'd have to do it himself and grinned as he said it. Soren was in his early seventies by then. Amelia had left him a decent chunk of money (much to Morris' disgust) and the bunkhouse to live in for the rest of his days. Then Soren said it was wrong but he would take care of it.

He rode off in the direction of the pine bluff on Amelia's horse and neither was ever seen again in Goodland. They just vanished together. Wade said he remembered him being a tall, slow-talking, kind man who spoke Swedish with his Grandma and who helped with Grandpa Gavin when he was going through a patch of shell shock.

Penny wishes, for at least the hundredth time, she had known Amelia Larson Toland, the woman who loved this land and horses too.

*   *   *

I remember a long hill.

I checked my brakes at the top and I could see buildings a long ways off, on either side of the highway.

It wasn't running right. Could have been the motor, I just couldn't tell. The vibrating started up again, and a new grinding noise. I'd never heard or had any kind of experience with either symptom like that on the truck before and it was frustrating. I'm not that mechanically minded or able or whatever. Norman might have known what it was but I'd left him behind and it was new to me. I just babied it down that long hill and pulled into the station on the right, Rocky Road Repairs.

I was held up four hours. He said I'd gotten some dirty fuel and he had to clean the lines and then some fiddling with the fuel pump. $280 on Visa later, I crawled onto the highway again. The Rocky Road mechanic hung up his Closed sign and burned past me in his three-quarter ton, headed, he'd told me, up to Fort Nelson for two weeks of hunting. Gotta get his moose, he'd told me.

Well, I stalled out completely on a flat stretch less than a mile away.

I suppose I was lucky to get towed back to the station on the left. Red Rock Station. First thing in the morning, he said, muttering in his beard and sending dark looks across the highway at the Rocky Road outfit. I wanted to phone home then but the pay phone was vandalized and this grumpy guy wouldn't let me use the grimy phone in his station for long distance. He knew I was desperate and he was the only show in town. He was just a cantankerous, anti-social sort and he didn't care one whit about me wanting to call home or any non-business stuff like that.

I believe I begged.

Three hours and $320 later, with a second-hand alternator and maybe five dollars left on Visa, I got going again, with the truck still running a bit too rough for my liking. But I wouldn't stop. I was mad, I remember, because those bills just about killed the joy out of my profit margin. I would barely make it home on the fuel I had left.

Did I say I'd dropped off the honey?

Did I drop the last of it off?

I must have. Well, I guess so…sorry, I keep repeating myself, keep forgetting stuff, wanting to call home, forgetting all over again…

*   *   *

Friday morning, 9:10 a.m.

The phone call is brief and to the point, just like Guy Chevrier. They'll fax the agreement and if she would sign it and fax it back immediately, they will start excavating that afternoon. They need access through the fence line and they will confine excavation to the site inspected by Chevrier.

Fine, she says, that sounds fine. She'll grant access and if they need a wider gate for their equipment, which they did, they are responsible for building the gate to suit their specifications.

And Penny has a quick, grateful weep right there in her cinnamon-scented kitchen, taking pumpkin muffins out of the oven before going to the office where the fax paper is already chugging through their old machine.

The company needs one hundred and twenty-five loads to start, and that could be it. Never mind. Penny signs the document and sends it back. She'd done her homework and they are paying the going rate for gravel. She cannot imagine Wade objecting but it is too late now.

The deal is done and she has just saved the Toland Ranch for at least the next eight month's worth of bills. She blows her nose and laughs.

She has to go to the cemetery at 1 o'clock this afternoon to see the headstone for Margaret Rose and Morris put in place.

Morris Hamilton Toland
b. 1932 d. 2000
Son of Goodland pioneers

That's all Wade could come up with. It wouldn't be proper to say "R.I.P. you old fool." "Beloved father" would be a lie as would "Loving husband" or "Doting grandfather." This is the most accurate, fair-minded epitaph he could think of and it will do for all eternity now.

Margaret Rose Toland
b. 1937   D. 1983
Loving wife & mother

Penny stands in the freezing cold and watches Mort Granger, Mr. Sexual Innuendo of the Co-op Bench set, deftly operate his front-end loader to lower a wide slab of smooth grey granite over Morris' raw earth and then neatly maneuver the pink granite headstone between both their graves.

On the right hand side were Gavin and Amelia Toland and beside them were two smaller headstones. Son Daniel, killed overseas in France in 1944 and daughter Eva, killed in a car accident in 1952. Neither had married. Eva had been a nurse and she'd also worked overseas during the war. Morris, ten years younger than Eva, had no stories or memories to share about either of his older siblings.

This strikes Penny as sad and odd and useless, all at once. Morris was the only child left to inherit the ranch and he seemed to have grown up as the self-centred apple of his otherwise sensible mother's eye. Gavin had died in 1968 of a heart attack so Morris was all the family Amelia had left. There was Soren, of course, her best friend, but Morris had forced his hand within hours of Amelia's death.

Morris was a sad, scared old man. He didn't have a very happy life and his own self-centred personality didn't help matters. What did Dad say? "Life is what we pick and what we are dealt and what we make of both". Yes. Whether it's good looks, good health, inherited wealth, a happy marriage and family life, satisfying, well-paid work or satisfying poorly paid work...or the very opposite of all the above.

Penny stands, freezing, musing. She realizes Mort has finished the work and is waiting for her to snap out of her reverie. She thanks him very formally, without a trace of a smile, avoiding eye contact, and gives him her cheque for the Goodland Cemetery Society. She drives to the Co-op to buy coffee beans from Evie and a large bag of dog kibble for Casey. Surely Wade will be home tonight. She has a couple of steaks thawing for dinner and she splurged on fresh mushrooms and store-bought Romaine lettuce for Caesar salad, his favourite.

Coming past the cemetery on her way back home, Penny toots the Dart's asthmatic horn on impulse. She laughs at herself but she can imagine Morris rearing up with that belligerent look on his face and then Margaret Rose's firm, pleasant voice telling him to just lie back down and stop bothering other people.

And perhaps now, Morris will meekly obey.

*   *   *

First there are snowflakes, big fluffy ones, fluttering down from the sky and patting his face. Little wake-up calls.

He tries to move but when he starts to push himself up, the potatoes give way like ball bearings and he rumbles down a steep slope with spuds rolling under him and bouncing all around him.

It takes many long seconds for this mixed cargo to stop but Wade faints again and doesn't feel the extra bangs his broken body absorbs en route.

When he tries to get up again, his right arm is impossible to bend. It hangs off his elbow at a weird angle. It is hard to breathe through his nose because it is broken, too, so he sucks air in and blows it out through his bleeding mouth.

The stink of diesel and smoked rubber and burnt potatoes swirls around him in a foul smog. He figures out that he must be down in a big ditch or a coulee bottom. It is dark, so dark he can barely make out his left hand when he gingerly swings it up in front of his eyes. 8:20 p.m. according to the shining green dials of his watch. His eyes hurt with the effort of deciphering the time. His head hurts all over. He stands up.

He thinks he hears a motor.

The high arc of light nears but when he turns his head to look up, the searing pain nearly drops him to his shaking knees. The headlights advance high above him, illuminating the shale cliffs above the highway and gleaming briefly on the steaming wreckage scattered down the impossibly steep slope between himself and the highway.

He stands, waiting for the driver to notice something, anything at all, like the smoke lingering in the air but the lights and the motor of the diesel pick-up recede, leaving him weaving in the dark.

He puts out one foot and nearly falls. There is nothing there but air. He slowly kneels down and puts his left hand out, patting the rocky ground. A crater of some sort and more potatoes. Or is this an apple? Wrong shape for a potato. He feels something tightening around his head and tastes fresh blood inside his mouth. Fighting it, breathing now, taking deep breaths, he carefully stands up again, shifting his weight from side to side, thankful that both knees and ankles seem in working order.

It is cold though and the snow keeps falling and he feels himself trembling. He tries to pull his jacket closer, fumbling with his left hand for the metal snap buttons.

Wade stands there alive in the dark.

Nobody else knows he is down here.

*   *   *

The RCMP cruiser moves slowly down the unfamiliar country roads, toward the white wall of the storm which is swallowing the entire valley, blanketing the trees and fields on either side until sky and land merge into a shifting mass of greys and whites.

A steady wind, forerunner of the first major Arctic cold front of the season, pushes through the yard and behind the fence where cattle stand, hump-backed against the north wind, chewing their cuds in that patient, unflappable way they have of enduring nearly everything. She can barely make out the shapes of the horses sheltering on the lee side of the two long hay sheds.

As she'd driven down Samson's Hill, coming back from the Farmer's Market in town, she'd seen the cattle and the horses in a long dark line, all trudging toward shelter and food. Even though she was happily tired after selling nearly everything she'd made and every single pumpkin, even though she'd wanted nothing more than a quick supper of crock-pot stew and toast, she'd known what she had to do first.

The smell of the first incoming blizzard of the year is a pure, clean smell that pinches the nostrils and fills the lungs with a rare kind of cold, blue air. Ozone, she thinks, that's ozone. She gulps it in as she runs from the car to the house. Ignoring Casey except for shouted greetings, Penny runs up the stairs to the porch. Throwing Wade's chore jacket and her own coveralls on over her town clothes, grabbing the lined leather work gloves and jumping into her beat-up Sorel winter boots, she races for the barn, glad for the powerful yard light in the waning daylight. Casey runs behind her, delighted, his eyes gleaming, his grinning teeth shining.

She fills the row of water troughs first, cursing the antiquated system that sprays her several times. That will be fixed with duct tape tomorrow at first light, she swears. Properly insulated plumbing would have to wait another year. Then she runs for the tractor, grateful the hay pick is attached. Wade must have done that before he left. She needs to get six rounds of hay distributed beneath the lean-to shelters before opening the gate and letting in the cattle and the horses.

After a few fumbles, she regains her co-ordination with the levers to operate the system and spears the heavy rounds of hay. She wheels the tractor around briskly and transports the rounds, one by one, across the yard. There she loads them into the feeder plates and uses her knife to slice the twine, releasing the sweet summer smell of dried oats and brome and alfalfa. One of the cows begins a rhythmic bawling, setting off all her hungry sisters as well.

Food Want Food Want Food!

Penny smiles at the familiar noise-making and swings the tractor around again, heading for the hay shed. It takes her nearly an hour with the water and feed distribution. Now there is a regular din of bellowing, bawling cows, mad for the fragrance of good food and water and soon, dry straw to sleep on.

"Hang on you lot! I'm going as fast as I can! Put a sock in it!"

Finished with that job, she jogs over to feed and water the pigs and to shut the chickens up in their quarters. She treats Mister Bojangles to oats as well as hay and three carrots. When she finally opens the wide pole gate, he whinnies loudly and trots out of the horse barn to greet his long-lost lady friends as they prance into the yard well ahead of the cattle. All is well. She keeps an eye on the young stallion but he seems more interested in sampling the new food than challenging the aging sire. She whistles Casey to her side and gets them both behind the fence.

Then the cattle flow in, two hundred of them, some of the young heifers at a trot, bucking a little, and sensing excitement. The older cows and the two bulls head straight for the lean-to shelters and the hay. They know the drill. Others go to the water troughs first. The snow is coming down too thick and fast to do any kind of inspection or exact head count. She'd get to that tomorrow too.

Gratified, she turns to the house and that's when she sees the RCMP cruiser at the gate. That's odd, she thinks, we never see them down here. Are they lost?

Has Sherwin Evers finally done something illegal enough, beyond merely sleazy, to get himself arrested?

Casey barks a couple of times and then whines, pressing close to her knees, getting in the way as she walks over.

The older one speaks after taking off his hat. Penny stares at the snow falling on his grey brush-cut. Casey leans into her legs again and is silent.

There has been an accident. The truck totalled. In the Pine Pass. They will let her know as soon as they have confirmation of his whereabouts.

Whereabouts. What a funny word. What an odd thing to say, she thinks. No, he never phoned. Maybe he tried but I was teaching in town all those days. Yes, I've spent a lot of time away from home this week. The Farmer's Market today…

Yes, we do have an answering machine, but it's not working. It hasn't been working for a while now. The tape got all tangled up and I didn't realize it had…and the phone lines on this road weren't working yesterday, something about upgrading the service.

But it was knocked out for nearly half a day and well into the evening. I didn't even realize it wasn't working except that a neighbour told me today when I was in the store.

I went to bed early last night, just past eight o'clock.

No! I was home alone. Our two kids are both away at university.

The officers stand there asking these questions, the snow falling thicker and faster, both giving me a searching sort of look when I say no, you haven't phoned. They wait for me to say more, as if any good, normal husband would have phoned his wife at least once or twice during a nine day road trip. Here I am blaming the phone company. I couldn't afford a cheap answering machine even if I did have the time to look for one this week. Wade has the Visa card for fuel, for emergency repairs.

I am embarrassed for you. How thoughtless you must look to them but they don't know how much I've been away, how I've been so busy lately. The female officer asks me if there is anyone close by who can come and stay with me.

I say yes, there is, I will phone them right away, and I leave it at that.

What would I say to anyone? How can I phone Gwyneth and Gordon? What on earth would I say to them?

"Your father is missing. No one knows where he is. But our truck is burnt to a crisp. Not him, just the truck. No sign of him or that Norman. Please come home and wait with me."

As if there is anyone in the world except you who could explain this to me and sit with me and wait with me and make me understand what is happening right now, which is unbelievable. I just don't believe this is happening.

As if I would *want* to believe any of this.

*   *   *

They aren't smiling. The older white one with short grey hair and the younger brown one with thick black hair pulled up into a tight topknot watch me with wary eyes. I try to say something but I croak instead.

I hurt all over. My head feels like a vice-grip has

seized it and is gouging my skull from my ears up. My eyes water when I try to tell them about my head.

The older one tells me to lie still and close my eyes. She spoon-feeds me some sort of broth, good and salty, and has me sip warm water. She puts drops from a little brown bottle in the water. The vice-grips ease away from my skull and I try to say thank you but all that comes out is a strangled gurgle. Then sweet relief.

I wake up and smell salmon cooking. I am ravenous. But my thirst is the worst thing. My tongue feels like a swollen chunk of line-dried bath towel. I drink the water they bring me through a straw until my tongue feels almost normal. Then they feed me mashed potatoes, salmon cakes, apple crisp with Bird's custard on top and lots of hot, sweet tea.

"You from that truck wreck?" asks the younger one. Her voice sounds like she's from Jamaica.

"I guess I am," I say in my rusty-sounding croak. My jaw feels tender and there is a big wad of tape holding my nose in place.

"You have a dislocated shoulder, a broken collar-bone and some ribs cracked," says the older one. "And the nose. Broken too. So far as I can tell. But I want to keep a watch on that head of yours. Can you see clearly?"

No wonder I feel so beat up.

"Yes. The light hurts a bit though."

The younger one moves the kerosene lamp back behind her and the soothing shadows are back. I close my eyes but remember my manners.

"You've been taking care of me? Thank you," I say to them.

Her sharp eyes soften a little.

"My wife? Does she know I'm here?" I start to sit up but stop, my ribs squeezing the breath out of me. "You have a phone?"

They look at each other but stay silent.

"Phone? I have to phone home, I'm late, she'll…"

"No phone, no electricity, no TV, none of that," says the younger one.

"But how long have I been here?" I ask.

"Two days," says the older one.

I settle back onto the pillow, stunned. I look around again, seeing the log walls, the wood stove, kerosene lamps, open shelves with food supplies in tin cans or glass jars. A sturdy-looking door leads outside. I vaguely remember being helped out to pee in the snow. The other doorway, curtained off in heavy cloth with old-fashioned flowers on it must be for a bedroom. I am propped up with three pillows on a long couch beside a wood heater, tucked into a big down sleeping bag. It looks just like my old sleeping bag.

"Home sweet home," says the older one, scrutinizing me again. "Speaking of which, you could write your own ticket, you know. Nobody survived that wreck."

I stare at her merry brown eyes. What is she saying?

"Callie and me, I'm Grace, we walked away from bad wrecks ourselves. Your wife's Cicely?"

"No! Not her! My Penny, she's…"

"Oh," says Grace. "Well, that's different then. At least you weren't yelling at her. Anyway, you walked smack into our woodshed and, pure luck, Callie found you half-frozen on the ground the night of the snowstorm. She went out to get more wood."

"How'd I get here? I don't remember walking. I must have frozen solid."

"I'm a nurse and Callie is too. We bandaged you up here instead of trying to pack you out in the snow storm. You walked a long, long ways that night, going downhill, following the dry creek bed. You were in some shape. Nothing froze but you were hypothermia on legs. You're one lucky tough guy, for sure."

I nod but then, having spoken her piece she abruptly turns away and helps Callie with dishes. I close my eyes and think.

How can I get them to send a message to her?

She'll think I'm dead. Fried in that wreck. I saw the smoking hunks of my truck all over the place. Penny will take it hard. And the kids. Oh God.

Oh no, this is not too much to ask, for them to get a message out as soon as…as now. She'll be thinking awful things. My truck wrecked…

This is crazy. I've got to get out of here.

"Please?" I croak as loudly as I can.

They turn as one and stare at me.

"Please, I've got to ask you, please, to get word to my wife. Number in my wallet, my I.D., look."

Callie's eyes narrow but Grace looks thoughtful. They turn their backs again and whisper for several minutes.

"One condition, mister."

"Wade. Wade Toland."

"Yeah, we know that. Well, we don't want you saying anything about us or where we live or how you came to find us," says Callie.

Grace shakes her head ever so slightly. "Callie here,

and myself…have left a couple of bad fellas, ex-hus-
bands actually, far behind us and that's where we want
them to stay. We've managed for nearly two years and
we don't want anything to blow it. It's life or death to
us and I'm serious when I say that. It'll be big news for
you to have survived that crash and we can't be part of
the news in any way, shape or form. Understand what
we're saying here?"

"Yes, ma'am, Grace, Callie, you can. You have my
word. I'll just say I…I lost my mind or something and
can't remember a thing," I say, "It's not so far from the
truth. I have no idea where this is, this place of yours,
and if you think I can travel, I will…"

"No. You need to rest up a while longer. Just say a
couple angels came to your assistance after you had a
big bang on your head."

"Throw in a white light and a long tunnel and
they'll run for cover and leave you alone," says Callie,
and grins for the first time, lovely white teeth in a
pretty chocolate brown face.

We all laugh except it hurts when I do, with these
damn sore ribs. I am wrapped up like a mummy with
my arm and shoulder and ribs. And my nose and my
head, all broken. Grace checks me over and then she
helps me get up and out to their outhouse. This takes a
long while but I emerge, finally, shaky but relieved. No
obvious signs of internal bleeding. Grace demands to
know this before I stumble back to the cabin with her
holding me up.

The sun is shining and the snow is starting to melt
fast. I can hear chickadees and nuthatches singing in
the dense bush surrounding their cabin. It's a beautiful

late fall day and the world is recovering from the first snowfall of the season and me, I'm alive and recovering too.

They tell me their stories and I tell them mine in bits and chunks as things come back to my mind. I sleep a lot, thanks to the little brown drops in the water they give me. We stay up late one night when I am feeling better, drinking coffee with rum in it, listening, talking. I know my stories are jumbled, what I remember of this trip, the delivery stops, everything. Grace says I have retrograde amnesia, common in head injuries.

"Temporary condition," she says in her lilting Jamaican voice. "Don' you worry."

I cannot remember the crash at all. I just remember driving in a blizzard, again. I have one memory of a runaway lane heading up a hill at the bottom of a big curved stretch but I don't know where that's from or when. It's frustrating not to be able to think properly. I know I've taken a runaway lane at least twice before. They may look rough but they are built in all the right places and they do the job, save you from piling up.

Grace says that most everything will come back to me but some things will take time. The main thing is my vision is clear and my head doesn't ache as badly anymore. She says I must be patient and count my blessings.

"Some things are better forgotten anyway," Callie says, and we have another sip of coffee and rum to toast that home truth.

Then it's time for more little brown drops and another good night's sleep for me.

I wander through the house with Casey behind me, whining softly in his enquiring way. I sort of notice that he's inside but I pretend not to notice because I need someone living and breathing and warm inside this house. Wade is seriously allergic to cats and it is such a shame because with all this hay stored nearby, we have mice aplenty. And they can be such good indoor company, cats I mean, not mice. It's too cold to keep cats outside up here in the north. People do it but it's cruel, no other word for it. Poor animals. I'm rambling. I know.

It doesn't make sense at all. When you're on your way home, you call from somewhere, to say you'll be three hours or one hour and do I need anything in town? This, if the timing is right, or put the steaks on, honey! Again, depending on the time of day, just to give me notice, unless it's really very late, then you just rumble in the driveway. But if it's the middle of the day, I go about my business and keep an eye on the clock and sometimes Casey and I walk up the road allowance and I'll pick wild raspberries and wait for the first little dot to become the familiar bulk of the truck on Samson's Hill.

"It's him, Casey, it's him!" I'll sing out and Casey will twirl around in a couple of enthusiastic circles, barking little yips, looking in all directions, not exactly sure why but willing to play along with me.

Then he'll hear your motor, long before I can, and his fake yips to humour me will become joyful bugling and sometimes excited and inaccurate peeing, which is always something to keep an eye out for.

So he's allowed inside tonight, Casey is. He'll hear you coming down the road and he'll let me know, no matter what time it is, I just want to know.

*   *   *

Remembering they brought me here, Callie and Grace, some days ago. 'Time you need to prepare yourself, Wade. Time to think. You'll be fine,' one of them said. Then nothing but the sound of their Jeep truck and the rough, jouncing ride for hours and hours. I'm packed in the back in my sleeping bag, curved next to the cab. There are pillows and rolled up blankets all around me so I can't move. Then we hit too many potholes and I holler because it hurts like hell to be thrown into the air and especially, to land. Bring on the brown drops. Put me down.

Waking up here. The fire just dying down, a neat pile of kindling and split wood beside the small barrel heater, an old-timer. A large yellow enamelled tea kettle is hissing away quietly on top of the heater. I'm wearing my underwear and T-shirt in my sleeping bag on a built-in bunk with a thin mattress. My clothes are in a neat pile on one of two rickety wooden chairs right beside the bunk. It's bright daylight so I get dressed. I don't know where my watch is.

A slim stainless steel thermos and a squat red plastic thermos are on a card table, along with a plastic bag with homemade bread and some ginger cake in it. I drink the hot mint tea from the thermos and eat some of the cake. Delicious. Then I open the red thermos and find warm ham and bean soup and I devour that too. A wonderful soup. Penny makes it too. I never tire of it.

This is a different cabin, smaller than Callie and Grace's. Someone seems to live here, at least sometimes. There are cans and glass sealers on the shelves above a built-in counter. Tea-bags, two cans of ground coffee, eight cans of Carnation evaporated milk, sugar cubes in another coffee can, oatmeal in a restaurant-sized coffee can, another large one labelled biscuit mix and another half-filled with cornmeal. Sealed glass jars with strips of beef jerky and dried soup mix, five cans of pork and beans, four cans of corned beef, even a large glass jar of sauerkraut. No peanut butter or jam. One nearly full glass jar of orange marmalade. If I'm careful, I can last a week or ten days. I push the clean blue gingham curtains aside to look out the window and all I see is snow.

I nearly miss the cloth bag under the grocery bag. Two freshly sharpened pencils and a pad of white paper.

I put two more pieces of wood in the heater and check the water in the kettle. It's at the half-way mark, nearly boiling now. Fine. I sit down with the pad of paper and the pencil. HB, nice and dark. The paper is good too, a bit of heft to it.

I want more tea so I use two of the black tea bags and add them to the steel thermos and then pour water in it from the whistling kettle. Toss in some sugar cubes too even though I usually take it black. I crave sweetness.

Doodling away, sipping tea, feeling good. Page one of the

sketchpad looks like a three-story tree fort. Advanced architecture it's not but there it is, my doodling.

I gave them old salvaged nails to straighten out and boards from the oldest granary that finally had to come down. The kids built the fort that summer...hours of building and playing.

I flip the page, feeling silly. Want to write something down, not draw amateur pictures. I drink more tea. I should write the most important things I can remember. So I know who I am when I'm cornered, when I'm trying to remember.

'For the fearful and the rigid, change means defeat. They'll live on sickly-sweet, half-frozen potatoes, wrinkled turnips and diseased wild rabbits rather than leave the farm to earn money. They'll demand that their children quit school by Grade Nine and go to work cleaning other people's houses or motels or go shovelling grain or swamping gas field trucks, afraid their own children will be bright and talented, will outgrow them and see them for what they really are. Completely limited by their own ignorance.'

Who said that? My mother? Was she telling him off? He wanted me to quit that young? No. Doesn't make sense. Who then? Who? Does it matter? No. Yes.

I'm hiding behind the kitchen door listening to the adults and they are talking about neighbours...Evers! They're talking about Evers and how Sherwin has to leave school at the end of Grade Eight. Mother is mad about it. She's visiting with Georgie Lemieux. It's the spring before she got sick. They both feel very sorry for Sherwin. They've seen a good heart in him somewhere. He's fourteen. I'm thirteen.

"When the prairie chicken drags her wing and limps away from you, humour her. Follow along for a while, walk slowly in the same direction. She's play-acting for her babies' lives so don't go looking for the nest and don't let the dog get anywhere near either."

Grandpa Gavin, holding my hand, teaching me about nature on our long walks down to the breaks. I must have been six or seven then. He died not long after.

My right hand is sore. Stiff. It won't go away when I flex my fingers. I feel like I should lie down. I'll do more of this later.

Draw things. Find things to remember. Write them down.

Help me keep things straight in my head. Who I am, who my people are.

*   *   *

I can't tell the kids, not yet. It could ruin their year, I mean, it will ruin their lives. They could fail their first term exams. All that time and effort and now, who could begin to concentrate on mid-terms with a father missing, presumed dead?

The police haven't released his name to the news people. I've begged them not to, talking about next-of-kin and notifying everyone. They have his photograph, the one close-up photo from the last family portrait we did, for the media in case someone remembers seeing him and the sooner, the better. The "truck wreck and miss-ing driver's" story is playing on most television stations, they tell me, but they are withholding all names.

This is a bad movie.

Thank God they're both at university, far, far away from this. I'm not in my right mind.

Frederic phones. He wants to thank me, again, for having his senior class out digging clay. He says it's practically pure, that clay. A few drops of icy rain were falling off and on that day, the same day I made the gate. Frederic is happy, he says, because less than two hours of digging resulted in four hundred pounds of clay, enough for the rest of the year's art classes. Right there in a thick seam on a side-hill so steep we could never safely go near it with farm equipment. We always looped around it.

Frederic is still chatting away. It will appease the school administration who seems alarmed at the thought of the art department, which is him, one teacher, needing a fuel and supplies budget for the kiln which hasn't been used by an art teacher for six years. But he is a potter. That's what he does, makes pots and platters and mugs and giant vessels, he says.

Frederic is jolly. I am numb. Free clay. Giant vessels.

Then Frederic tells me that he will forever have an image of me riding up to where they were digging, after I'd taken them to the clay bank and then gone off to make the new gate. That he wishes he'd had his camera to photograph me all bundled up, with my tools in the pack on my back, and Maggie May high-stepping. Says I looked like I'd ridden over from a Western movie set.

I say, Oh, because I am numb, too numb to be flattered by this romantic image-making for my benefit but unable to just say, Stop. Then he invites me to accompany him to the school's Halloween dance. He's signed up to chaperone but no one else is volunteering. What a bunch of killjoys, he declares, what a bunch of stiffs on that staff. But he would love my company. He finds the staff a bit cliquey and not really all that welcoming to a single fellow. And he doesn't play basketball so the men think he's a dud. So would I keep him company and help chaperone?

I am so shocked. He's never directly asked me if I was married but I think I've been obvious, mentioning Wade and "we" and "our ranch" and so forth. I'm wearing Margaret Rose's wedding ring plus my engagement ring from Wade on my left hand, for Pete's sake. Why is he asking for my company? I'm a substitute teacher with no obligation to chaperone at that school and furthermore, I'm a married woman.

Have I been sending him some sort of signal? Am I being some kind of obvious lonely woman?

No, he fancies himself too much to find out if I'm at all available. Just springs it on me, out of the blue when I am already in shock.

I bark at him that there is more to life than dances. Some of us have livestock. I say I'm expecting my husband home any minute now.

I am over the top. Over-reacting. But it's too late, I've said it.

He says, very softly, sympathetically, "'Oh, it's like that, is it? Pardon me, I really didn't mean to upset you, Penny. I've obviously misunderstood. I thought we could be friends, pals, fellow craftspeople sort of thing, nothing heavy. I'm very sorry."

So he hangs up.

Now he'll think I'm a redneck philistine hick who

can't even decline a normal school function gracefully and he'll leave me alone for sure. I flee to the bathroom for a strange little weep. I have never cried so much in years as I have this past two weeks. Stress, never-ending stress. Even though I know better, I feel like I brought this on myself and I am ashamed. He wouldn't ask me to a dance if I wasn't giving off hormonal signals of some kind, would he? Or am I getting mixed signals from him? I think so. I do.

I've fended off Morris, that randy old goat, and that creepy Sherwin Evers, but I know damn well I wasn't being the least bit inviting to either of them. Wade knows nothing about his awful father. Evers we can joke about. But Morris? That would have killed him. No, Wade would have killed Morris and that's what silenced me.

It hung in the air between us, Morris and me. He respected me for it, he said and he didn't try anything again after that. I told him I would chop his hands off if he ever came near me. I was twenty-two and just barely pregnant with Gordon. Wade had gone off again somewhere in the truck.

I shouldn't have had to deal with that by myself.

But I did. He just looked, after I told him off, for years, just looked. I wanted to shower with a Brillo pad some days, just to scrub the tracks of those hungry, needy eyes off me.

But I didn't want Wade to lose this land. Not because of his father's lack of morals.

I didn't want to lose this land. I loved it too much by then. We'd added our initials beneath all the courting ancestors on the big old poplar tree on the breaks.

G.E.T. + A.L.T.
M.H.T. + M.R.G.
W.W.T. + P.G.B.

Three generations of jack-knives had raised dark grey welts in the pale green bark of the poplar. For true love, tradition had it that the initials had to be carved while the carver sat on the back of a horse. The live totem of youthful and enduring affections in the Toland clan.

When Morris died, neither of us cried, not once.

We'd grieved his mother, cried in each other's arms and it bound our hearts together right from the start. Wade has a good, gentle heart and I knew then I could trust him, forever, absolutely.

But there was no grief for Morris and only disgust and anger when we found out what he'd done. Even the old lawyer looked apologetic. The bank manager looked afraid for us, folding and unfolding his hands, awkward in his stiff new suit.

But what on earth am I going to do now? I need to work in that school.

Just ignore him. He's just trying his luck. He's lonely.

Liar, liar. Once you start, you can't stop.

So, he's very attractive. Anyone with eyes can see that.

I am numb all over.

But he reminds me I'm alive, inside.

He can tell.

I've got enough real problems to deal with before I start creating more of them. Get a grip. It's been nearly twenty-four hours.

And my husband is not missing! He's somewhere, out there, alive if only someone would find him!

I've done the chores, glad for the distraction of the animals and the cold weather. I've had to crank up the furnace. I'm burning wood in the kitchen stove just to warm this place up.

I don't think I can face the vehicle insurance people about the truck or the bank manager about the mortgage insurance for the same reason. They will want a death certificate. I am trying to think, trying to be practical. Wade is missing.

I'm not going near that new John Deere fellow. I think the insurance people will be the most straightforward to deal with first. The RCMP report verifies everything. Except for the obvious.

As if Wade would desert his family or be some kind of contrary, hard-to-find corpse.

I try to think.

Tomorrow morning, if I don't hear anything, I will phone the kids and we'll figure something out. Tomorrow.

I try to run the home movie of Penny Loves Wade, Wade Loves Penny, but his face is not right. He's not looking at me, he's distracted, he's chewing at his thumb, he's fidgeting with his ear. Now he's doing that nervous jaw thing he's been doing for the last few months, opening his mouth up wide to relieve his tight jaw muscles. I've told him to see the doctor but no, he won't. He doesn't even know how much he does that. It's a grim little hippopotamus habit now, isn't it?

Oh God, what on earth am I thinking?

I know I'm in denial. I am freezing my heart and

mind until it's safe to go crazy in the privacy of my own home. To wear his old T-shirt with the faint, good smell of him to bed again and try to sleep, but I can't sleep at all. To wish I hadn't done the laundry so I had more of his old clothes, more of his smells left to me. I have held every shirt and sweater and pair of underwear to my nose for the past hour, trying to find him.

I will finish the special quilt I started so many years ago and have it ready for Christmas. Thirty-six squares, most of them made already. PENNY LOVES WADE. And at the bottom, for my freezing toes, WADE LOVES PENNY. Because he is a regular furnace with nice warm feet and I've never had cold toes since I got into bed with that man.

Has he deserted me, in cahoots with that Norman, made it look like an accident? Is that what's happened?

I can work all night if I want to. Nobody else needs to know.

Maybe I should phone the kids. No. Not yet. But I've got to talk to someone. Oh God, my poor old mother will finally have a disaster worthy of the name to be gloomy about. This will put her over the edge, it will, because all her dark predictions about Wade and the trucking business will have come true at last. He will have left me in the lurch, just as she predicted. I cannot stand to think about what she will say so I won't call her until I absolutely have to.

My brothers? No. We exchange Christmas cards. Sad but true. What do I know about them anyway? What do they think of us besides telling me endless silly farmer's wife and traveling salesman jokes? We were never really close to begin with, six and eight years older than me, and we've grown even farther apart. We have next to nothing in common with each other as adults. I like my sisters-in-law a lot but I don't really know them, not enough to invade their lives with this kind of news. Not yet.

Hazel Collins? No, I can't do this to her. She taught my kids and we do neighbourly favours for each other but this is too much, too heavy.

I don't have a best friend here anymore. Not since Sally and Glen moved off the farm eight years ago. I could phone Sally but what would she do? She's in Armstrong growing peaches and cherries, happy as can be. What could she do? Say how sorry she is for me? Of course! Who wouldn't be sorry for me?! I don't want pity.

I want to know where Wade is.

There's nothing anyone can do until we know what happened to Wade. Nothing will comfort me except knowing that and then I've got to be brave for Gwyneth and Gordon.

I've got to be strong and see this through. I don't have a dozen nearby close friends or family to be with me. The Good and Toland cousins are all much younger or much older than us. I've been too much of a homebody to do anything but join the choir and the Historical Society and I can't load this news on anyone there. I wish Sally lived closer. I'll call her. Tomorrow.

He is lost or something even stranger, even worse.

*　　　*　　　*

When I open my eyes again, I can hear someone at the door. The knocking must have woken me up. 'Hold on,' I say, 'be right there.' But the knocking and bumping noises don't stop until the door is shoved open just as I'm kicking free of my sleeping bag.

The familiar musk of his aftershave and the unholy stench of his rotting body combine and all I can do is yell, 'Hey! Hey! Get the hell outta here!' and grab the poker by the heater.

'You're my son, godammit!' it bawls back and starts to move toward me but I raise the poker and it stops.

The sagging, peeling face contorts into something I can't make sense of until I hear it croaking and crying. 'You gotta know I'm sorry, so sorry, boy. I just need to say I'm sorry. I wasn't good. I know.'

I am getting rushes of goose bumps up and down my legs and I keep edging away from it, gripping the poker hard.

'I just wanted my Maggie Rose. That's all. She could see the good in me, only her. And when she died, what little good there was of me died too. Except you. She left me you and I couldn't care for you. Same green eyes as hers watching me. I just couldn't care for anybody, even you, without her. Forgive me. You're my son. Please.'

And then his corpse is on its knees wailing and I'm standing with the poker dangling from my left hand.

'No!' I yell. 'Get out, get out now!'

'I hated my godamn life, boy. I hated that ranch and the stinking goddamn animals and everything about the place. But I stuck it out. Made a living. Thought I could hit the jackpot and leave it for good. Give you a big chunk of money first. Forgive me, forgive me, please!'

I shake my head and that's when it grabs the poker out of my hand.

'Sucker!'

It's Norman. Norman Deville. He waggles the poker at me. He's hale and hearty and it's nobody else. It's that sonuvabitch Norman.

'So hit me, Wade. Give it your best shot, ya gutless wonder. Slinking around this place like I wouldn't notice. Stand up like a man for once in your life, ya stunned…'

I grab the poker back while he's yapping. I grab it and swing at his head and miss by a mile. When I manage to get the poker from my useless right arm to my left, Norman is the rotting Morris corpse again and it's wailing and begging but this time the poker connects with the skull. And I yell and yell and whack it again. And I yell myself awake in a heaving sweaty tangle.

The shack is ice cold. My clothes are folded neatly on a three-legged chair beside the bunk bed I'm lying in. There is a slim stainless steel thermos and a short, wide red plastic thermos on the floor beside the chair. I ease out of the sleeping bag, holding my right arm close to my chest. I'm still protecting it but the sling is off now. I stretch the arm out very slowly and carefully. I get dressed quickly though because the place is freezing and snow is drifting in through the broken window beside the bunk beds.

I brush aside the flapping, colourless rags hanging across the broken glass and survey the view. All I can see is blowing snow. The land is snow. The sky is snow.

Impossible to tell what time it is. I turn around to see what I can make of this place.

It reeks of packrat. Even with my broken nose, I can make out the musky pong of the rat. There is an ancient rust-covered barrel heater in the centre of the room, a built-in counter running along one wall and two shelves above it. There are a couple of tin cans, one filled with rusty nails, and two broken glass sealers grey with spider webs on the shelves. Along the opposite wall are the built-in bunk beds, four of them. There are no mattresses on any of them. There are mouse turds everywhere. The Hanta Virus Hotel.

On the spikes driven into the wall by the door are my lined jean jacket and a black wool toque. I don't recognize the toque. I used to have a cowboy hat. I don't seem to have it anymore. This wool over my ears will do the trick.

There is a new pair of leather mitts with wool liners tucked into the pocket of my jacket. I put them on as well as the hat because it is very cold in here. I have to take the mitts off again to open the steel thermos. There is tea, something green and medicinal but it's good even if it's lukewarm and I drink it, all two cups of it, one after the other. I am thirsty as well as cold. I investigate the red plastic thermos and find a bean soup with a bit of ham, barely warm but definitely tasty. I finish it off as well as two thick slices of some kind of ginger cake. It fills my empty gut and I feel much better and stronger now. I find my watch and a pack of water-proof matches in my inner coat pocket. It is 2:25 p.m.

Time to head outside. I need wood and I need to know where I am. I put on the jacket and head out into the weather for a good thirty metres before I stop and look back. This shack is almost certainly an old cowboy line shack, nearly at the top of a high valley ridge. The valley is short and wide but it looks barren. The few trees that are standing don't have branches and are fire-blackened. Standing deadwood. I can barely make out the narrow double tracks of a road looping from the valley bottom up to the shack. And there are three whiter than snow circles on the valley bottom. I stand for a while, shivering and pondering before it comes to me. Alkali lakes. Dried up alkali bad water lakes. No wonder the shack is abandoned. Can't graze cattle where there's no good water and poor grazing as well. It must have been a better place at one time.

I move around to the lee side of the shack to inspect a slumping pile of wood blocks and notice that rainwater must have run off the rusty tin roof and onto the pile. The big chunks of punky, charred wood are glued together with ice. I kick at a few of them but it is obvious that it's terrible wood, good only for adding to a roaring bonfire. They are still in big rounds and there is no axe in sight.

I look harder and spot a single-bit axe with a broken handle less than a foot long, tucked overhead between the wall and the tin roof. The rusty axe head is as loose as a six year old's front tooth as well.

I decide to pee while I'm out here scouting around and head over to a small stand of young poplars just about my height. They must have grown up after the fire. I'm hoping for some fallen dry wood, thin enough to break over my knee. Campfire wood. No luck.

But when I'm zipping up I hear the sweetest sound.

The sound of a big rig downshifting very close to me, just over the ridge which is less than fifteen metres from me to the top. It sounds like it's rounding a long bend, then shifting down, hiccuping down a longer hill, braking and shifting down again before making another sharp bend.

I start moving back to the shack to collect what's left of my stuff.

*   *   *

"Murphy's car went over the bridge before anyone knew the far end had been swept away by the ice-jam on the river. He was tossed out, no seatbelts in those days, and he clung to a chunk of ice which delivered him close enough to shore for him to climb out. Murphy could not swim. He emptied his boots and scrambled up the banks, just in time to stop a bus from crossing."

"Mrs. Nielson's husband formally deserted her and their nine children after the war, which he had run off to join, covering up the fact that he was forty-two, a farmer of sorts and the father of nine dependents. She operated a dairy, Goodland's first, and every child had to milk two cows, once they were ten years old. The littlest ones churned butter by hand and they pressed it into wooden boxes with a flower pattern carved into the wood which showed up nicely on the pound of butter. They sold it at the Goodland Co-op and traded lots of milk with their neighbours for hay and oats to keep the cows going. She made the girls dresses out of flour sacks and the boys all had Five Roses brand shirts as well! Mrs. Neilson lived to be ninety-three years old, with more than fifty grandchildren and nineteen great-grandchildren. Don't know whatever happened to the old man and his English tart but I hope he suffered and died slow and that's about the kindest thing I can say about the glory-seeking old sonuvabitch."

"Jules Leyton was only fourteen when he arrived in this country, tagging along with the Heinrich family from dried-out Saskatchewan. He married Karla, their youngest daughter, when he was eighteen. He was out proving up his homestead and at that time, you had to clear fifteen acres annually. Jules had a strong young back and an axe but he had a lot of bush to get through. The open prairie land with a few sloughs on it had been snapped up by the first arrivals so the heavy bush was left to the late-comers. He chopped into his leg near the end of one day, tired of course, and he hollered until he couldn't yell anymore, tying up his wound by tearing up his shirt and making a tourniquet about the slash. He had his father-in-law's horse out with him, skidding trees he'd felled.

Karla was taking their dry clothes off the line and she got a funny feeling. So she decided to meet Jules who should be coming home for supper soon enough and she started out on the trail to the field he was trying to make. She found him bleeding to death and out cold. Karla was sixteen at the time but she rewrapped his wound (Jules just missed his artery, lucky thing) and put him on the stone-boat which was nearby, another lucky thing, and she hauled him up to the neighbour's. Mrs. Casson had been a Red Cross Outpost Hospital nurse before getting married and raising a family so she knew how to clean wounds and was no stranger to the damage done by axes and knives."

*   *   *

"Penny?"

"Yes, yes, it's me, Mum."

"Oh, good! Of course it's you, what am I saying? I've just been, oh the last couple of days, having a terrible worry-fit about you, you know how I get, and I just thought I'd better give you a quick call, make sure everything is all right, you know?"

"Oh, Mum!"

"What is it? What's wrong then?"

"Something just terrible has happened to us…"

"Don't go packing it about all by yourself, go on then!"

And so Penny spills the beans, with pauses for their separate and mutual weeps, and with Gladys consoling her and demanding that she herself call Gwyneth and Gordon and the rest of the family, offering to pay for their flights home.

"The biggest mistake of my life, of the many mistakes I've made, mind, was keeping your father's prostate cancer from you kids," Gladys declares. "But he wouldn't have it worrying you kids, 'interfering with their lives and all', is how he put it. As if your own father dying was some kind of noisy car passing you by on the street and backfiring, interfering with your afternoon peace and quiet. Well, I never should have listened to him and I know all three of you would have liked a proper last chance to really talk with him, any normal person would, but no, he was dead-set against it. Very private person he was and you're a bit like that too, Penny. Yes, you are. I know what it's like to go carrying around a big load like that, keeping it all secret about your father but for the doctor, like, and so that's why I say, let the people who love you know. Be honest about it and let the chips fall where they may but at least treat them like adults because they are. Now, I'll call Gordon and Gwynnie to tell them that it's not certain about their Dad but that they ought to get home as fast as they can. I'll spring for the tickets. Gwynnie and I can fly up from Vancouver together. That's not a problem. I insist. I'll let your brothers know as well. Right then, Pen?"

Penny says, "Thanks. I love you, Mum."

"Well, of course, and I do you as well, girl!"

Which they haven't said to each other in at least twenty-five years, if not longer. It's been hard between them. Chalk and cheese, that's the two of them.

She feels shaky but relieved and more than anything, grateful that she has just heard rare good advice from her own mother. She is gratified by that, feeling supported for once instead of harshly judged and found lacking. She drags herself to the bathroom to splash cold water on her face and prepares herself for the calls from Gwyneth and Gordon.

They might not believe their dotty, bingo-addicted Grandma who never could seem to remember their father's first name. Penny takes a deep breath and then another.

They call within five minutes of each other half an hour later. They let Penny know which flights they'll be on, and question her, disbelief in their voices, both frightened. Gordon reports that Grandma had been sharp as a tack. Gwyneth says she was really sweet and calm and organized. It is a minor miracle that she's been able to reach them both so quickly. Once again, Penny sends out a telepathic hug to her little Mum, careful not to mess the immobilized and resolutely auburn Margaret Thatcher hairdo.

Then she phones the RCMP in charge and lets him know that the next of kin have been notified and that the photograph of Wade she'd given them could be used for the media alert now.

They have no news about Wade but they are in-vestigating the other driver, who was last seen in Kam-loops but is now missing as well. Is she able to answer a few more questions?

Adrenaline rushes up and down her arms and legs in sheets of prickles. The lights in the kitchen seemed to flicker in front of her eyes and she sits down heavily on the high kitchen chair.

"Go ahead," she says.

Norman Deville aka Norman Mansour aka Ned Mason, originally Ned Mahone, wanted for theft, armed robbery, drug trafficking, smuggling. Dishonorably discharged from the U.S. Army. No record of ever having served in Vietnam. Prison record from 1965 to 1969 then disappearing from the States with an outstanding warrant for his arrest.

"No, we did not know any of that. Oh God," says Penny, phone jammed against her ear, white-knuckled.

"Your husband wasn't aware at all of this man's past?"

"No, no! He wouldn't have hired him had we known this. Wade is a straight arrow, a good man, honest and... no, we didn't know about any of this criminal background."

"Okay, then. You'll let us know if he contacts you right away, won't you? Would he have been paid in advance for this work? If he hasn't, he may try to contact you."

Penny feels her heart pumping in a ragged rhythm and she breathes, breathes again to cool her brain, slow her heart and lower her voice.

"I'll let you know, absolutely. I want you to find this man. If he harmed Wade, if this is what's happened, to make it look like an accident...is this what you think?"

The officer says something but Penny's brain is filled with the sound of her heart hammering and she stands up to look for the cheque book. She paws at it with one hand, riffles through the last two weeks of stubs, looking for a cheque made out to Norman but there is none. The officer is still talking and Penny strains to focus, to hear words in complete sentences.

"We are eliminating possibilities at this stage of the investigation, Ms. Toland. But you received no phone calls from your husband this entire time, confirmed by your phone records. Your husband's Visa was last used for what looks like two separate vehicle repairs about two hours east of Prince George."

"If you find out anything or come across something odd, please call me. Maybe it'll make sense...maybe I'll recognize something, you know?"

"Yes, will do, Ms. Toland. Take care now."

His voice sounds regretful, consoling. Obviously they think Wade has run off on her, had it planned right from the start. Penny starts to feel herself coming unglued again. She runs into the bathroom to do something about her aching eyes, a quick, cold cloth might help, and then, she cannot help herself.

She screams at the sight of her silver-white hair and collapses.

*   *   *

They must have driven me a very long way from their cabin and taken the back roads too. This is not the north, not the thick bush near Summit Lake or further into the Pine Pass where I think I was close to when I crashed the truck. This is the Cariboo or west of it. Chilcotin maybe. Dry ranching sort of terrain in the rain shadow of the Coast Mountains. Has to be!

I don't blame them, not really. I must be well enough for them to just leave me up here. I know I wasn't in my right mind at first.

Too many little brown sleeping drops?

I was imagining all sorts of things.

Had to be, none of it could be real.

It's just an old abandoned cowboy line cabin in the middle of nowhere.

*   *   *

She uses the computer to find the garages on the

Yellowhead Highway. She calls the RCMP but of course, they've already done that. One garage is closed for holidays. They are trying to find the owner but he's off on a hunting trip with some buddies. And the other guy doesn't remember anything out of the ordinary, apparently. A routine alternator job and adjusting the fuel pump. And towing. He had to be towed there.

Please, oh, please.

No body. Nobody.

I think that's good news.

Even if you don't want to come back here, you're alive. I just know that.

I believe I'd know for sure if you weren't. You're mixed-up, confused, angry maybe. Not dead.

You'd come to me then.

You'd say good bye to me somehow at least.

Damn it, Wade, you said you'd phone. It was the last thing you ever said to me.

*   *   *

Gladys's & Gwyneth's & Gordon's List

1. Hazel- phone tree for food donations & drop-off depot
2. Mort- on standby for cemetery crew
3. Aloysius, Georgie & Barbara- organize benefit event within 2 wks. Goal-$5,000 plus
4. Lou & Yvonne- organize roster for Toland chores if needed

5. Marjorie & her Lexus- chauffeur, airport duty
6. Lonnie & Cory- bring split firewood down to
Tolands, 3-4 cords
7. Judith, Father Murphy, Dorothy G. & Pastor
Raymond- prayer circles
8. Edna & Gwyneth- track down Toland and
Good cousins and relatives
9. Chester- contact Wade's trucking customers &
old-timers hockey gang
10. Francine-rehearse choir -standby for funeral
confirmation
11. Gordon-speak to Evers and to RCMP if he
tries to contact your Mom again about selling the
ranch to him

*　　　　*　　　　*

I am beginning to understand the squeeze chute of my
life, how I milled around home like a young bull,
cavorting on the river breaks, before being herded back. I
was pushed through a series of corrals, each one smaller than
the one before, until I was prodded into the narrowest
chute. Grim shock has set in for decades, you might
say. Branding, castration, dehorning, vaccination…the
whole process administered with some low-grade
anaesthetic so I could drift along, function "normally".
But I kept my sanity, I did, and I count my blessings for
a good woman, one tough enough and sweet enough,
too, to stand up to me. And for those two babies, those
fine twins of ours. My father could not take that

accomplishment or my happiness away from me. He left this earth bitter and broken and ashamed and I don't intend to do that to myself or anyone else I love.

*   *   *

Blue. Navy blue velvet for the main background colour and fabric. Gold, in something stiffer, cut on the bias, for highway stripes on black velvet to form the highways around the squares.

Nine by nine inch squares. A queen-sized quilt.

Bees flying among the letters: PENNY LOVES WADE. WADE LOVES PENNY. Honey bees toting a banner, pale blue sateen, with those letters, our names, for these fine new squares for the top row.

Today the envelopes arrived. Not a word inside, just three cheques. I told the police. Said I'd hand over the envelopes to them for their investigation. But I needed those cheques and I had to process them as soon as possible for the apiary's share as well. I'd let them make photocopies of them if they wanted. Yes, they did want them.

*   *   *

I tell the trucker to drop me off at the junction even though he's gone far out of his way already. I need to walk the next few kilometres home just to unkink my

legs and my back and think through the way I will
walk through the door.

*   *   *

Let me spread this out. Appliquéd sloughs, full of a
million bugs and mallard ducks and white-tail deer
drinking in the spring. Fringed with water-loving wil-
lows and the rich chestnut brown of cat-tails peeping
over their broad leaves. Spring in the sloughs. Birds
flying north in big ragged V's overhead and this one
with a pair of red-winged blackbirds singing that sweet
gurgling song of theirs.

And this one of the Canada geese and mallard
ducks landing on the sloughs for a rest.

*   *   *

The weather has warmed up a little, the snow has stopped
and I can see our road just fine in the dark with the
moon nearly full.

That driver was happy to have helped me out.
He'd seen my truck wreck back there in the Pine Pass
and wondered about me. He says all the drivers talked
about it on their CBs for days.

It's too close to home for us all, he said. Doesn't
know how anyone could walk after a wreck like that.
Never heard on the news if I'd made it or just what-all.

I'm a lucky, lucky man, I tell him.
He shakes my hand.
Good luck.
It could be catching.
We laugh about that.

*   *   *

Summer squares next. Pale yellow oat stubble in this wide-wale corduroy, draping perfectly over all the hills and hollows of the south-west quarter. Trapunto technique. Summer fallow in brown fine-wale corduroy. Hay in nubby thick green wide-wale corduroy going the other direction. Good solid colours, a soothing rhythm. Plainsong in cloth.

Autumn tweeds, flecks of orange against the deep greens and charcoals of spruce and black poplar trees. The breaks, the Muddy River, the coulees, all done in appliqué. Mum and the kids have just let me sew and sew while they look after everything, answer the phone, cook all the meals and do the chores if they're up before me, which isn't often.

I've been stitching our life together for days now… years, really.

*   *   *

I keep on walking and it sinks in that I'm wearing my cowboy boots which aren't good at all on slick, hard-packed snow. I move to the side of the road to walk in the deeper snow left by the grader so I won't slip. Instead, I stumble on the bigger frozen chunks of snow and gravel. My feet are ice-cold already and I'm starting to wish I'd taken the trucker's offer to drop me off right at home. But I've made the last hill.

And there it is. Every single house light is on. I know every room that's lit up from where I stand.

*   *   *

Winter. White velvet swathing the trees, the fields, and the aerial view of the ranch buildings. Add some of these little rhinestones for frost, yes, add lots, to the trees, the snowy roofs. All four of us bundled in winter coats waving. Casey beside us.

Oh God. Please, please find him. Bring him home.

*   *   *

I should have phoned home, I kept trying, but the line was busy every single time. We need two separate lines or a cell-phone. I'm going to insist after this. We have to have some other reliable way of getting through to each other.

The truck insurance money should help us. It will at least give me some time. Time to mend my body, time to plan a new life, to build a cabin on the breaks maybe, just for the two of us. If Penny will have me back after all this mess.

If this big, old mutt doesn't knock me down and slobber on me till I drown, that is.

Good dog, Casey, good boy!

*   *   *

Imagine stopping there in the snow, looking through the big bay window of the living room where she is seated at the sewing machine, working on something blue and gold. The faithful dog still dances around you, welcoming, ecstatic. The snow begins to sift down again, landing on your denim jacket like icy rhinestones and you are so cold, but you want to look at what home looks like just a little longer.

*   *   *

You are cutting the last bits of thread on the quilt you've been working on nearly non-stop for three days when you stop, put the material down, bow your head and will your spirit to reach out and find his, somewhere, lost out there.

*   *   *

A tall fair-haired man and a petite dark-haired woman bounce down the stairs and into the room, sweeping the air with their arms, taking turns holding up the large, beautiful quilt for the others to admire, hugging the small, white-haired woman.

These are your grown children. Gordon and Gwyneth, but who...Gladys?

She brings a tea-pot and a tray of cups and cookies into the room, her hair still a bouffant helmet of dark orange.

Penny, her cropped hair a strange gleaming white, turns and looks right at you then.

*   *   *

Your eyes are so tired they feel poached in their own sockets. You think you are seeing things, hallucinating. It happens. Grief and longing do bring into being the ghosts of your life, fleeting glimpses of your father usually, but this thin, hunched man outside, he is still there. You want to open your mouth, tell the others to look but you cannot speak, you can only hold both arms toward the wavering reflection in the window.

*   *   *

Now, you turn and hobble up the front steps.

*   *   *

You are home now, is all you can say to each other at first, as you hang on to each other, leaning into each other.

You're okay?

Yes, you say, it is all okay.

You're really okay?

Yes, you are.

You are safe.

You are home now.

ACKNOWLEDGEMENTS

Thank you to my stalwart friends, family and colleagues who never doubted I would finally see this novel in print. Blessings on all your fair heads and good hearts! Grateful thanks to Randal Macnair of Oolichan Books for choosing to publish it and being wonderful to work with; ditto for my editor, Ron Smith, with an able assist from Pat Smith, for astute editorial work. I am honoured to have Marilyn Harris' lovely, perfect painting, 'Prairie Quilt #2', for the cover. For their help with research in the Peace River country, I thank writer and community historian Louise Framst and librarian Marsha Triebner. Ernie Fuhr of North Peace Apiaries graciously showed me how to back up his big International truck and answered all my questions about hauling barrels of honey and other cargo. Any errors or omissions in this regard are mine alone. Sparing me the expense of getting my own air brakes ticket, I enjoyed the trucking adventures found in Big Rig, from New Star Press, written by veteran trucker and great storyteller, Don McTavish. For funds which allowed me time to research and write, I thank the Canada Council for their early and vital support. I am also grateful to friends who needed a house-sitter or a farmhand or who provided crucial time and space to write: Jim & Helen Wood, Cheryl Fraser & Mike Rouleau, Ann & Ron Thompson, Dr. Jennifer Dodd,

Mona Fertig & Peter Haase, Rita Moir in the era of the Vallican Log Palace, and the Bethlehem Retreat in Nanaimo. For their careful readings of earlier drafts of this novel, I thank booksellers Jenny Mitchell, Susan Lock and Angela McDiarmid, stellar publishers' rep Kate Walker, librarian Evelyn Goodell and librarian/novelist, Anne DeGrace. Finally, I simply could not have persisted with rewriting this novel had I not had the constant encouragement of poet, novelist and friend, Paulette Jiles, and the research and writing skills, love and support of Jeff George and of our son, Seamus, who has been asking about my "Odyssey book" for so many years. Thanks to you all, here it is.

Recipes From Penny's Kitchen

Best Rhubarb Punch

*makes 27 four ounce servings-make one day in advance of event

14 cups chopped rhubarb

4 cups hot water

2 cups granulated sugar

1/3 cup cold pineapple juice *vital ingredient!

6 cups cold soda water

Ice ring or block-plain or cranberry/raspberry juice ring

In large stainless steel pot, combine rhubarb and hot water. Bring to a boil, reduce heat, cover and simmer for 40 minutes. Strain into large bowl using a large, fine sieve. Return to clean saucepan and stir in sugar. Boil, stirring, for 3 minutes. Cool, cover and refrigerate for at least 3 hours. Just before serving, stir in pineapple juice, then place the ice block or ring in a large punch bowl, pour rhubarb mix over it and add cold soda water. Garnish each cup with a sprig of fresh mint.

My Friend Barb's Rhubarb Chutney

*Sterilize 8 half-pint sealers, lids and tops.

4 cups chopped rhubarb

2 ½ cups Demerara sugar

4 cups finely chopped yellow onions

2 cups white vinegar

1 tsp salt

1 tsp each of ground cloves, allspice, cinnamon,
cayenne pepper

Put all ingredients into a large stainless steel pot and
boil, uncovered, until mixture thickens. Pour into hot
sterilized jars and seal. Wait for 40 days and then devour
with cheeses, cold cuts, salmon, chicken, or venison.

Spicy Zucchini Boats

Preheat oven to 350 F. Lightly butter or spray olive oil into a baking dish.

Blanch 4 small or 2 medium-sized zucchini which have been sliced in half, length-wise. Blanch in boiling salted water for 2 minutes or microwave for 3 minutes.

Hollow out carefully with a spoon, leaving a quarter-inch wall.

In a small bowl, combine 4 oz. cream cheese, ½ cup grated Monterey Jack or aged cheddar cheese, ½ cup Parmesan cheese, ½ tsp. Sambal Oelek or preferred hot sauce on hand, 1 tsp fresh chopped chives. Add finely chopped zucchini pulp and mix well. Fill zucchini "boats" with this mixture, put in baking dish and bake for 8-10 minutes.

Zucchini-Lime Marmalade

* prepare 6 half-pint jars, lids and tops in boiling water bath

4 c. grated zucchini

2 c. water

½ c. fresh lime juice (about 2 large or 4 small limes)

1 pkg. Certo powder

6 c. sugar

3 tbsp. grated lime peel

First, grate 3 tbsp of lime peel, then squeeze juice to make ½ cup. Combine grated zuke, water and lime juice in large saucepan. Boil 10 minutes. Stir in Certo & boil for 3 minutes, then add sugar and lime peel. Boil hard for 1 minute. Remove from heat, skim off foam, and stir for 5 minutes to keep the marmalade clear. Pour into sterilized jars and seal. Lovely on bagels with cream cheese.

Caroline Woodward lives, works and writes on the Lennard Island Lightstation near Tofino, British Columbia. Prior to her career as a lighthouse keeper she worked in almost every aspect of the literary world from book-reviewer to book-seller and many points on either side and in between. She was raised on a homestead in the north Peace River region of B.C. and has studied, worked and travelled widely ever since. She is the author of five books including *Disturbing the Peace* (Polestar, 1990), nominated for the Ethel Wilson Fiction Prize and *Alaska Highway Two-Step* (Polestar, 1993), nominated for the Arthur Ellis Best First Mystery Award.